TO HAVE AND TO KILL

The Wedded Bliss Mystery Series
Book Two

Christine Lawrence

First paperback edition June 2025

Book cover design by Julia Stahl, Jules Creative Solutions

Editing by Ramona Mihairr

ISBN: 979-8-9910885-3-4 (paperback)

979-8-9910885-2-7(ebook)

To those who feel lost, or don't feel seen, I see you.

CHAPTER ONE

The Wedded Bliss, my family-owned wedding and event center, had been around since my mom and aunt opened it in the early eighties. My mother passed away when I was young, and my aunt Sissy became my guardian. Recently, she left us, and I am running the business now with my two best friends, Chelsea Baker and Meg Strickland.

A few months ago, shortly after I took over, The Wedded Bliss was in serious trouble, and to make matters worse, one of our grooms was found murdered. Thankfully, with hard work and determination, we managed to save the business, and with the help of a private investigator, solve the murder.

That was all behind us now. Today, October 25th, we were holding our latest ceremony. I shifted my gaze to the bride on my right. This one was the strangest of all the weddings we had organized. The couple's strong fascination with zombies and the apocalypse made it the theme for their special day.

"Jodi, now it's your turn," I instructed.

Wearing a torn and dirty wedding gown, and holding a fake black rose bouquet, she gazed directly at her soon-to-be spouse. "My love, I vow to fight by your side at the end of the world. And should you ever become a zombie, bite me so I can become one, too."

"Do you Jodi take Andrew to have and to hold from this day forward till the post-apocalyptic world?" I asked.

"I do," she replied.

"Andrew, do you take Jodi to have and to hold from this day forward till the post-apocalyptic world?"

The groom wore a matching, tattered white tuxedo. "I, do."

"By the powers vested in me, by the State of Ohio, I now pronounce you husband and wife in life and the afterlife. You may kiss your bride," I said, concluding the ceremony.

Jodi and Andrew kissed, zombie makeup and all, while the audience cheered.

The couple recessed, then the rest of the wedding party and me. Once they were back down the aisle, the ushers began dismissing the attendees row by row. The bride's group formed a receiving line in the hallway just outside the Cupid room. I greeted the guests briefly and then headed to the kitchen.

"Greetings!" I called out as I entered the double doors.

Rushing around a prep counter, the talented chef hurried

toward me, ready to give me a big bear hug. "Leah, my dear! How are you? How did everything go?"

"I'm good. The ceremony went well." I let out a chuckle. "It's not often you get to marry a couple that resembles zombies."

Stefan laughed and pretended to shudder. "I must agree. Trays with a skull in the middle covered in deli meat, BBQ meatballs as zombie's eyes, and mini smoked weenies are not my regular wedding fare."

I swatted my hand towards him. "Oh stop! It looks amazing. Even if it's a little untraditional."

"Thank you, now scoot, I need to get service started," Chef Stefan instructed.

Before walking out the door, I giggled while spearing a weenie with a toothpick. "I'm going."

After leaving the kitchen, I stopped back by the Cupid room. All the guests appeared to be enjoying the cocktail hour. The couple even created a signature drink called v 'The End of the World'. The area was draped in red and black fabrics, zombie-themed centerpieces, and the favors were mini apocalypse survival kits. I was a little hesitant when first meeting with Jodi and Andrew, but I think we pulled it off. A perfect theme for fall as well.

At the moment, I could see everything was going smoothly. Now it was time to focus on the wedding show being held this weekend. Chelsea had a connection with a local bridal magazine and offered our facilities for the event. At first, I was somewhat hesitant, but I must admit we pulled it together. Our theme was 'Destination Bridal' - a one-stop place to meet vendors from all aspects of the planning process a bride needs for her special day.

Meg and Chelsea were waiting for me in the conference room to go over last-minute details.

"Hey guys, sorry, I'm here. I wanted to do one last check and ensure things were going smoothly," I said as I entered.

"No problem, we've just been chatting. She fed Delaney and put her down for a nap," Chelsea replied.

Delaney was Meg's new daughter, only a month old. She was the sweetest. Since we were young, Meg always talked about getting married and having kids. She excelled at it. Chelsea was the complete opposite. She thrived in the single life, always out partying and usually dating whichever guy caught her eye that week. I stopped bothering to remember their names. But recently, it seemed like one guy was managing to keep her attention. As for me, I feel kind of in the middle.

Out of a serious relationship, but not quite ready to jump into another one. My ex and I were planning a future together. All that changed when I lost my job at the lab and had to come back home to take care of Sissy. He was focused on his life plan, and dating a small-town wedding planner didn't fit. A few guys caught my interest, but I was too focused on work now.

"Thank you for letting me bring her," Meg said.

I smiled at her. It was no big deal. "Of course. You know she is welcome anytime."

Chelsea cleared her throat. "If you all are ready, we can get started." I thought we would go over the schedule."

"Sounds great," I replied, joining them at the table.

"Tomorrow, vendors will arrive around to set up. There are fourteen in total, including us. We assigned five to each group, with the first coming at eight, the second at ten and the rest at noon. I figured it was better to stagger them, so there would be enough room for trucks and unloading in the parking lot," Chelsea explained.

"Smart idea. I am picking up the passports from the print shop in the morning. The proofs looked amazing, I can't wait to see them," Meg gushed.

"Did we already assign all the vendors a stamp?" I asked.

"Yes, that's all done. When every merchant arrives, they will receive a packet with a schedule, their booth assignment, food vouchers and their stamp," Meg explained.

"The large tan suitcase will be placed by the door, across from the front table, where attendees can drop off their completed passports on the way out to enter the grand prize raffle," Chelsea added.

"Awesome." I nodded. "I believe the brides are going to love half off a package here at the Wedded Bliss and an article in the Buckeye Brides wedding guide. Another table will be positioned there for the door prizes in the front hall.

Chelsea nodded. "Right. Friday, we open our doors starting at four p.m. until ten p.m.. Then begin at nine am Saturday till six p.m. and Sunday is twelve p.m. till five p.m."

I glanced over at Meg. "When do we have the décor, demo?"

She skimmed the schedule in front of her. "Saturday at four."

"Perfect!" I exclaimed.

"The only thing we'll have left to do is send the final agenda to the printers and stuff the goody bags. Buckeye Bride wedding guide sent us 250 of them," Chelsea said, holding one up.

"How nice of them. Those are cute," I commented.

"Sally already set up the various items to be stuffed so we can do an assembly line," Meg added.

"Let's get them knocked out. We'll wait till tomorrow morning to bring them up to the front hall. That way they are secure until then. Sound good?" I asked.

"Great idea," they chimed in.

We got to work stuffing bags. Each of the vendors submitted flyers, brochures and business cards. Others sent coupons for their services just for the brides attending the show. The makeup artist and hairstylist sent cute little mini lip balms and styling products. The baker made special individual cookies, while the DJ included a sample CD with the top five most popular wedding reception songs.

Once the bags were stuffed, I sent Meg and Chelsea home. The marriage celebration wound down and our staff began cleaning up and tearing down. The upcoming few days were going to be long and busy. We all made plans to meet before the vendors arrived.

The next morning, before my alarm went off, my brain was screaming at me to wake up. Groaning, I stood up and stumbled to the bathroom. Stepping into the tub, I closed the curtain and let the hot water beat down on me. As I opened my eyes and grabbed the body wash, I caught sight of a small lump on the tile. I quickly scooted and backed into the corner. I stuck my leg out cautiously and touched it with my big toe. Oh jeez, it was just one of the cat's mice toys! I told the girls about keeping their toys out of the shower, so I guess it's time to start closing the stall door now. Once I finished, I felt refreshed and more like myself, then headed back to my bedroom to slip into the outfit I had laid out.

After I got dressed, I trudged to the kitchen, grabbed some apple juice, a slice of cheese, and pulled out two slices of bread from the breadbox. Oh man, the fridge looked pretty bare, it was time to go shopping. I made a mental note that I would probably forget later. I slid the pieces into the toaster while I filled a travel mug with coffee. Once the bread was finished toasting, I placed the cheese in between and squished it down. When I was younger, it was the first thing Aunt Sissy would let me make by myself because I always woke up before her on Sundays and she was usually recovering from an event the day before.

Grabbing my keys and purse, I locked up and headed out.

Before the event, the Ashford Chronicle was sending over a reporter to interview us and write about the bridal show. Hopefully, the press will be beneficial. The traffic was light, so I made it to the Wedded Bliss in no time. The benefits of living in a small town. Our only real major traffic were ducks, farm equipment, and the occasional deer.

"Good morning, Leah!" Sally greeted me from the front desk.

"Good morning! Is anyone else here?" I asked.

"Meg just got here a few minutes ago. I haven't seen Chelsea yet. There are muffins in the conference room, and I started a fresh pot in the coffee maker," Sally replied.

"Great, thank you," I said, heading back to my office.

Placing my purse on my desk, I grabbed the folder for the bridal show and a notebook and headed to meet them. I was a little stressed that we would have enough people show up, but we made a commitment, and I trusted our team to pull it off. Meg was already waiting at the table.

"Morning. Are we prepared for this?" I asked, taking a seat across from her.

Meg smiled. "As ready as we can be."

"We'll give Chelsea a bit more time, then get started," I said.

"Sounds good," Meg replied.

A few minutes turned into fifteen and Chelsea finally showed up. I wish I could say I was surprised, but let's be honest, I would be more worried if she was early.

"Nice of you to join us," I murmured.

She scrunched up her face and stuck her tongue out. "Oh shush. You know me, I'll be late to my own funeral."

She wasn't wrong. I just shook my head. "Let's get started. We need to decide who wants to be positioned where. One person needs to be at the front table, one at our booth, and another one walking around making sure things are going well and be available in case anyone needs anything."

"I'd prefer the front desk or the booth if that's okay," Meg piped up.

"Chelsea, do you have a preference?" I asked.

"No. If Meg covers the booth, I'll take the front. It will allow me to keep track of stuff for accounting purposes," Chelsea replied.

I took down a couple of notes and then glanced up. "Sounds good. Now, as for Saturday and Sunday, do you want to keep the same posts or alternate?"

"Why don't we just play it by ear?" Meg suggested.

"Works for me. Anything else we should discuss or that we may be forgetting?" I asked.

"I'll be posting on our social media accounts during the show and taking video clips
of the different events. If you take any photos, send them to me," Meg instructed.

Even though she was a new mom, Meg was determined to give one hundred percent to her duties at the Wedded Bliss. I tried to convince her to slow down, but she was stubborn. She was a whiz with computers and social media. She spent the last two months creating our website and establishing a presence on all the big platforms. Something my aunt never did because she didn't understand technology. It appears to have paid off already to get our name out there.

"Great idea. Which reminds me, the reporter from the Ashford Chronicle will be here around eleven," I piped up. I may have sounded upbeat, but I was nervous I would stumble over my words.

Meg beamed. "Awesome. Between the article and social media posts, we should have a decent turnout!"

"Here's to a successful show. Team Wedded Bliss, we've got this!"

A couple of hours later, the first vendors were set up. So far, so good. While they were busy, Meg, Chelsea, and I were putting the finishing touches on the Wedded Bliss booth. Meg found the cutest little magnets, key chains, and pens to hand out with our logo and business info.

Once we finished, I decided to check in with my fellow vendors and introduce myself again. My first stop was Fannie's Florals. A longtime business owner, Fannie Harrison, was *the* expert in the flower world. Her booth was assigned to the Cupid room.

I went up to her table. "Morning Fannie, how's it going?"

Her gaze caught mine. "Oh, hi Leah. It's going well. I'm just staging my displays right now. My assistant, Wendy, is bringing the floral arrangements and centerpieces closer to the start of the show, so they stay fresh."

I smiled. "Great. What will you be showcasing?"

She moved her hands over the sections of her booth. "Here, in the front, will be six types of bouquets, varying from tiny and simple to large and extravagant to the more modern style made from brooches. Then in the back, there will be different-height centerpieces. From small glass bowls with floating candles to tall vases with Fannie and hanging crystal jewels."

"What great ideas! I think the brides will love seeing the variety of what you can offer. I'm going to move on, but don't forget to have your door prizes on the front table by three," I reminded.

"Not a problem. Thank you. I hope they do," Fannie replied.

Across the room was Elegant Bridal Artistry, a local hair and makeup salon. Lina Fuentes, the owner, was setting up two chairs in front of mini stations on either side of their area. On the main table sat pricing sheets and bookbinders.

"Hey Lina, it looks beautiful!" I declared as I reached her booth.

"Aww, thanks a lot. I have a lot more to do. When the models arrive, we'll get their hair and makeup done and they'll be ready for the fashion shows," Lina beamed.

"Perfect. If you need anything, please let me know. I'll be

walking around today," I stated.

"Thank you, I appreciate it," she responded.

I headed next door to the Love room. I looked around and was amazed by how well our team arranged the room for our travel theme. This would be the first room attendees would enter to start their journey through the show. The room was designed to look like an airport, with the door as an airport gate. Little planes, globes, and passports were hung sporadically from the ceiling. They even positioned chairs as if you were waiting for your flight.

One of the first vendors you visited was Hart to Heart Paper Company, which carried all your stationery needs from save-the-dates to thank-you notes and everything in between. The best part was that they could accommodate every theme and budget. On each end of her table were tall four-sided rectangular grid displays that rotated. Each side displayed different types of invitation sets.

"Hey, Julie. Your display looks amazing," I said.

Julie turned around. "Hi Leah, I think it's coming together. Thank you, I'm almost done."

"You're welcome. Hope you enjoy the show," I said.

Satisfied with what I had seen so far, I hoped things would continue to go smoothly. Checking my watch, the reporter would be arriving in about an hour, which gave me a chance to complete some work in my office.

CHAPTER TWO

T ime got away from me, and someone knocked on my office door before I knew it.

"Sorry to bother you Leah, but the reporter's here," Sally said.

"Great, show her in," I instructed, straightening up in my chair.

"This is Miss Walton from the Ashford Chronicle. Meet Ms. Jordan," she introduced us as she ushered the reporter inside.

A petite girl with dark brown hair and blue eyes walked through the door, dressed in a lovely navy-blue top and skirt, paired with black kitten heels. I stood, shook her hand, and invited her to sit.

"Thank you, Ms. Jordan," Trina Walton replied.

"Oh, please just call me Leah," I said, sitting down.

"Leah." She smiled. "Is it okay if I just jump right into some questions?"

I nodded. "Of course."

"Why don't you begin by giving me a little of the history of the Wedded Bliss?" she asked.

"Sure. The Wedded Bliss was opened in 1989 by my mom Susan and my aunt Lulabell. They wanted to provide a space for brides on the most important day of their lives. Over the years, it has expanded from two main event rooms to three indoor event rooms, a gazebo area, a garden, and full-service catering. My mom and aunt worked hard to build the business and now we serve brides from all over the central Ohio area," I explained.

"Do you offer any special deals or services?" she asked.

"We do. Recently, we launched our Bride-on-a-Budget packages, and our anytime weddings," I said.

Trina glanced up from her notepad. "What do you mean by anytime weddings?"

"For couples who wish to forego the big ceremony but desire something different from the courthouse. We offer short, simple ceremonies," I explained.

She nodded as she continued to scribble. "Let's talk about the bridal show this weekend. How many booths will there be?

I shifted in my chair and re-adjusted. "We are featuring

fourteen local businesses, including the Wedded Bliss, to help brides plan their wedding from start to finish."

"That's great. Is there a theme to the event? she asked

"Yes. The theme for the show is Destination Wedding. Each vendor will be a major stop or place a bride needs to consider along the journey for their special day. From invitations to flowers, bridal cakes, and all the important people in between," I said.

She sighed. "Aww, such a clever idea! What days will the bridal show be held and how much does it cost to get in?

"The bridal show will run this Friday four to ten, Saturday from nine to six, and Sunday from twelve to five. Admission is ten dollars and there will be a lot of door prizes and raffles. We will also have fashion shows and demonstrations throughout each day," I explained.

"Sounds like it will be a great time. Where can people find more information or a copy of the event schedule?" Trina asked.

"You can find The Wedded Bliss on our social media pages, Facebook, Instagram and our website. All the details regarding the show can be found there," I replied.

There was a knock on the door.

"Excuse me," I said, rising to open the door.

Meg poked her head in. "Hey Leah, sorry to interrupt, but we need you."

"Sure." I turned to look back at our guest. "Please excuse me for a few minutes. I'll be right back. Would you like a glass of water or a coffee while you're waiting?" I asked.

"No problem. Some water would be great, thanks," she responded.

I followed Meg out into the hall. "What's up?"

"The second group of vendors are setting up and Fannie has a concern that the people from Grand Lush Bridal Salon are impeding on their booth space. Would you mind going over there and trying to smooth things over?" Meg asked.

I nodded. "Would you mind getting Trina a water please while I am gone?"

"Of course, not a problem."

I headed down the hall to the Heart room. As I got closer, I could hear yelling. Oh no. Running down the hall and into the room, I found Fannie nose to nose with a tall supermodel-looking woman with a huge chest.

"What is wrong with you?" Fannie exclaimed.

"My dresses are one of a kind! They need room to be openly displayed," the model looking woman shot back at her.

"You're already over into *my* booth area by three feet!" Fannie exclaimed.

"Excuse me ladies, if I may interject here. Please lower your voices. Then let's all take a deep breath. Will one of you please tell me what is going on?" I pleaded.

Fannie pointed her finger towards her opponent. "Ms. Mitchell is trying to take over more space and encroaching into my booth area."

Ms. Mitchell rolled her eyes and huffed. "I am simply placing the dresses with proper spacing, so they can breathe and be showcased as the elegant dresses they are."

"While I understand both sides, your booths and displays are an integral part of the bridal show. How about a compromise? We can move the décor from the left side of the bridal salon's space and put that between the two booths. Then Ms. Mitchell can expand her display on the other side," I suggested.

Fannie nodded vigorously. "Sounds good to me."

I turned towards Ms. Mitchell. "Will that work for you also?"

"Please call me Vanessa," she instructed. "That would be perfect! "

"Good. I'm glad we could come to a resolution," I replied.

"Thank you again. I appreciate it," Fannie replied.

"Annie!" Ms. Mitchell bellowed.

A very shy girl with brown hair, big glasses, and a drab green and tan outfit came running from around the corner.

"Yes ma'am?" she responded.

"I need you to move on this side to the other end," Ms. Mitchell directed.

"Of course, right away," Annie replied before scurrying off.

"If everything is good now, I'm going to head back to my office. I'll have one of my staff members come move the décor," I advised.

When I arrived, Trina was still waiting. "Thank you so much for being patient. Where did we leave off?"

"No problem, I think we're pretty much done. I would like to take a few pictures if that's okay?" Trina asked.

I nodded and smiled. "Of course. What did you have in mind?"

"Would it be possible to get one of you and your staff?" Trina asked. "Then one of the rooms for the bridal show and some shots of your facilities."

"Sounds perfect. Let me get Meg and Chelsea and we'll head back up front," I instructed.

The reporter followed me down the hall. We had a very nice sign on the wall near the entrance with our name that I thought would be the perfect background. Below was a great picture of my mom and aunt when they first opened the Wedded Bliss.

Our secretary, Sally, was sitting up front.

"Would you mind paging Meg and Chelsea? Trina would like to get a picture of us. Also, can you please see if Chef Stefan is available?" I asked.

"Sure, not a problem, dear," she replied.

While we waited, I glanced over at the front table we set up for the show. The goody bags had been brought up, name tags, and schedules were set on the table along with the passports they would each receive. A few minutes later, Meg, Chelsea, and Chef Stefan joined us.

"Great, everyone is here. Would in front of this sign be good Trina?" I asked.

"Perfect. Why don't you all stand behind the desk," she suggested.

We lined up behind the desk. I was in the middle. Chelsea and Chef Stefan stood to my left and Meg and Sally to my right.

Trina raised her camera and pointed it at us. "Are we all set?"

"Ready!" we replied in unison.

Click. Click. Click. She brought the camera down and glanced at the screen. "Great, those look good. Thank you so much!"

"Thanks to all of you, I appreciate you coming up," I said.

"Of course," Chelsea said.

They all dispersed, and I led Trina outside to explore the two outdoor spaces. I started with the left side of the gazebo area, which was painted white with a dark gray shingle roof and shaped like an octagon. In front of it, there was enough space to set up twenty-five to fifty chairs for guests.

Once Trina took a few pictures, we headed to our garden. The wedding aisle was lined with short green bushes. At the end, stood a beautiful cherry-stained wood arch that was big enough for the couple and officiant to stand under. On either side, there was enough space for fifty to sixty guests.

Trina took several more pictures. "These are gorgeous spaces. Thank you for showing me around."

Whew, that wasn't as bad as I thought. "Of course, my pleasure. Let me walk you out," I replied.

Once Trina left, I returned to check-in with more vendors. The front was abuzz with activity. Boxes, carts, and all kinds of items were being brought inside. Poking my head into the Heart room, it was coming along.

I offered to pick up lunch for Meg, Chelsea, Sally, and myself. The girls gave me their orders, and I headed to Gibson's Deli. We each ordered a sandwich and one large antipasto salad to share. A popular spot in Ashford, it was always hopping. Luckily, another customer was leaving, and I snagged a spot up front.

"Hey, Leah. Long time no see," Jessica called out as I walked in.

She always made you feel like family when you came in. "I know. I've been so busy getting the bridal show together. How have you been?" I asked.

She smiled. "Great thanks. What can I get for you?"

"I need a pastrami sandwich with Swiss on rye, a turkey breast sandwich with provolone on white, a roast beef sandwich with cheddar on wheat. and a ham with cheddar on white," I read off the list.

She glanced up from her notepad. "Anything else?"

"Yes, we need a large antipasto salad with extra Italian packets," I replied.

"Sounds good. That will be $34.27," she said.

I handed over my credit card. She swiped it and handed it back to me. I took a seat while I waited. I began scrolling on my phone and checking my socials. According to the local community Facebook page, the elementary school was holding a Halloween bake sale, the junior league was gearing up for its holiday bazaar, and Ed Hagerty was picked up again for public intoxication.

Once my order was ready, Jessica called me back up. "You're all set, Leah. Here are your sandwiches and salad. Do you need plates and silverware?" she asked. "I already put some napkins in the bag."

I didn't even have to ask. She knew I was a messy eater. "Thank you, those would be great."

"You got it. Good luck this weekend. You'll have to let me know how it goes," Jessica said.

"I will. If anyone you know is getting married, send them our way. Lots of great vendors will be there," I responded.

She waved. "Of course. Have a good one!"

"You, too!" I called back.

Lunch was amazing. The remaining vendors got all set up without any more issues. The next few hours flew by, and it was time to take our positions for the show. I made a final walk-through of each of the rooms to make sure everyone was ready. Thankfully, they were. It also appeared that things between Fannie and Ms. Mitchell were squashed.

Back at the front, I gathered Chelsea, Meg, and Sally together. I was still nervous about pulling off the show. Looking at my team, I knew I was worrying for nothing. Each of them had worked hard to make this come together and I couldn't be prouder.

I passed out a bottle of apple juice to each one. "Are we ready?" I asked.

"As ready as we're going to be," Meg replied as she raised her bottle.

"Always ready," Chelsea beamed.

"Here's to a successful show and happy brides!" I exclaimed lifting my bottle

"Here, here!" Meg and Chelsea chimed.

"Cheers!" Sally added as she tapped her bottle against ours.

CHAPTER THREE

For Friday, we had a decent turnout. About thirty-four of the fifty goody bags set aside for tonight were claimed. As I walked around, I saw happy brides and busy vendors, it was amazing.

Our first bridal fashion show was about to begin. We had set up a small T-shaped runway in the back half of the Cupid room. The show would open with wedding dresses from the Grand Lush Bridal Salon. After the earlier incident, I wanted to make sure everything was ready to go.

I found Vanessa backstage. She was dressed to the nines in a fitted black sheath dress with dangly diamond earrings, a matching necklace, and bracelet with high heels. Her hair was up in a French twist. If you didn't know better, you would think she was a model herself.

"Hey, I just wanted to check in and see if you're all set," I said.

She didn't even look at me. "I believe we are. Making a few minor adjustments. Some of the models are not as svelte as I was expecting,"

Stunned, I didn't even know how to respond to that. I bit my lip before I said something I may regret. "Good luck with the show."

I quickly left to check in with Reese Mason of All Occasion Entertainment. Not only was he one of our vendors, but he was also providing music for the fashion shows. Fairly new in town, he became one of the most sought-after dee-jays around central Ohio. It didn't hurt that he was young, tall, dark, handsome, and built like a Greek statue.

"Hey, Reese. Are you all set?" I asked.

Reese glanced up and gave me one of his stunning smiles. "Yes, I was just doing a last-minute test of the microphones and speakers. I think the playlist I chose will be perfect."

I clasped my hands together. "Awesome, I can't wait to hear it. If there's anything you need, let me know."

"Thanks," Reese said.

The fashion show got off to a great start. The ooh's and aah's from the audience made my heart happy. I headed out of the room to catch up with Meg and see if she needed relief. She was talking with a bride and her friend.

I waited till they finished. "Hey, Meg."

She grinned. "Pretty good turnout, right?"

"I agree. I can't wait to check in with Chelsea about the numbers."

"Are you okay if I head out soon?" Meg asked. "I'm a lot more exhausted than I thought I would be. And I'm sure my hubby is ready for a break."

"Of course. I think we'll be fine. I'll go ask Chelsea to come to relieve you."

She smiled and rose from the booth. "Thanks, I appreciate it. I'll see you guys in the morning."

"See you then!" I headed back up to the front. "Hey Chels, how's it going?"

"Great!" she exclaimed.

"How many tickets did we sell?" I inquired.

"The total count was sixty-seven," Chelsea responded.

That was awesome. At first, I was a little unsure if things would work out. "No way!" I exclaimed.

Chelsea smiled. "This is only day one."

"Meg needs to head out early. Would you be willing to cover the booth?" I asked.

"Sure. Let me lock up the money box in the office and I'll head over," Chelsea replied.

"Thank you. I'll clean up the rest here, so it's set for tomorrow," I offered.

After things were in order, I continued down the hallway,

when one of the brides stopped me.

"Excuse me, do you work here?" she asked.

"Yes, I do. How can I help you?" I replied.

"I just wanted to say thank you for such a great evening. My mom and I are enjoying ourselves."

"Thank you. I'm so glad to hear that." I plucked one of my business cards from my pocket and handed it to her. "If you have any questions or need anything from the Wedded Bliss, please let me know. I'm Leah, the owner here."

"I will. Thanks again."

All the time, planning, and stress were worth it knowing we made someone's day. The rest of the evening flew by. So many happy brides and happy vendors. Hopefully, tomorrow will be as successful. Chelsea and I closed up and went our separate ways.

Once inside my house, I kicked my shoes off and removed my bra as I headed down the hall to the bedroom. I pulled out one of my favorite oversized sleep shirts and a pair of fleece pajama pants. I removed the clips from my hair and pulled it into a messy ponytail. I stopped in the bathroom and scrubbed my face. I felt so much better and comfy after the long day.

The kitties had found me and meowed their displeasure at the lack of attention. I reached down and petted each of them. They were soothed momentarily, but I knew if I didn't feed them soon, there would be mutiny. They followed me to the kitchen and watched me like a hawk as I pulled out a can of wet food and split it onto two separate plates.

As soon as they were taken care of, I began scouring the cabinets to see what I could eat. I settled on a can of ravioli and some bread with butter. Simple but delicious. When the microwave dinged, I grabbed the bowl out, placed it on the plate went to the front room, and settled in my recliner for a binge of my current Netflix show.

The next morning, I stopped at Tanner's grocery store and picked up donuts and muffins, and a mocha latte for myself. Today's show was even more jam-packed with demonstrations and fashion shows. I was looking forward to it.

As I turned into the parking lot at the Wedded Bliss, I noticed Vanessa Mitchell and her assistant. Her assistant was carrying so many boxes that she looked like she was going to topple over. Vanessa was walking ahead and didn't seem to notice or care Annie was struggling. Exiting my car, I hurried over to her.

"Morning, can I help you with any of those?" I asked.

Annie turned to look at me. Her glasses were falling, and she looked tired and disheveled.

She shook her head emphatically. "No, no that's okay, I've got it. Thanks though."

"At least, let me get the door for you," I offered.

Annie gave me a slight head nod. "Thanks."

I walked ahead of her and held the door. Once inside, she scurried off. I stopped off to see Sally.

"Morning Leah." She sniffed the air. "Is that what I think it is in that bag?" Sally waggled her eyebrows.

I held the bag up and waved it back and forth before placing it on her desk. "You know it, only the best."

Sally chuckled. "Oh, my. I know the doctor said I should watch my sweets, but I think I can make an exception just this once."

"They say diamonds are a girl's best friend, but I think they're donuts," I replied winking at her.

"You sound just like your aunt!" Sally laughed.

"Everything going ok so far?" I asked.

"Yes. Most of the vendors are here getting ready for the day," Sally replied.

"Great. I'm going to take these to the conference room. I'll see you later," I said.

After my caffeine and sugar fixes were met, I walked over to the Love room.

Scott Webb approached me. "Morning Leah. Sorry I didn't

get a chance to talk to you yesterday."

"Hey Scott, it's okay. I'm sorry too. How are things going?" I asked.

"Pretty good. We had a lot of interest yesterday. Brides were very interested in our varieties of ice sculptures. The biggest hit was our Eiffel Tower ice luge," Scott responded.

"Who doesn't love Paris at this time of year?" I laughed. "Do you have your presentation all planned out?"

"Yes, we have a special sculpture we decided to unveil just for this show. Garrett is going to bring it closer to the demonstration," Scott explained.

"Good idea. I'm going to keep walking around. I look forward to seeing your demo and it was good seeing you," I said.

"You too!" Scott called out as he walked away.

One of the most popular vendors yesterday was Stein's Jewelers. Mr. Stein has provided jewelry for many people over the years. His company was the go-to place for high school rings, and those looking for that perfect gift for someone special.

"Hey Mr. Stein, how are you doing?" I asked.

"I'm doing great thank you," he replied.

"How did yesterday go?" I asked. "Every time I came by you had people at your booth."

"It was wonderful. Things have been slow lately and it was refreshing to be so busy," Mr. Stein replied.

"I'm so glad to hear that. Your pieces are just so unique," I said.

"Thank you, not everyone appreciates handmade quality anymore," Mr. Stein commented.

"Of course. I hope you have a great time today," I said.

"Same to you. And Leah?" he called.

I turned around. "Yes?"

"Your mom and aunt would love what you're doing," Mr. Stein said with a smile.

I smiled back. They would, they really would.

It was time to open the doors. As I made my way to the lobby, I noticed Meg was already positioned upfront at the table.

"Did you and Chelsea change places?" I asked.

"Just for the first part, I thought we would. Is that okay?" Meg asked.

I nodded. "Of course, silly. Did you get some rest last night?"

"Yes, thank you," Meg replied. "I needed it."

I walked toward the doors. "Let's get this show started."

To my surprise, the line was already several people deep. "Welcome everyone! Come on in."

Attendees flooded inside, and I helped Meg at the front. Once things slowed, I left her and began making rounds between the rooms. The first of the bridal fashion shows was finishing in the Cupid room. Fannie was next with a demonstration of different bouquets, boutonnieres, and floral centerpieces.

A different demonstration occurred on stage for the first fifteen to twenty minutes every hour. This reminded me that I needed to check in with Katie on our décor team to make sure we were ready for our demonstration in a few hours. Finishing my last round, I headed to the event office to find Katie.

"Katie?" I called out as I entered.

"Just a minute please," she called back.

A few minutes later, Katie appeared from behind. "Oh, hey Leah, what's up?"

"I was just coming to see if we're ready for our afternoon demo. I would have checked in sooner, but I was helping Meg at the front," I answered.

"No problem. Yes, we're all set. We have some table settings we plan to display, a slide show of video clips and photos from previous wedding and event setups we have done," Katie explained.

"Awesome." I smiled. "Sounds like I had nothing to worry about."

Katie chuckled. "You just need to relax. We are ready and we'll knock it out of the park."

I sighed. "Sorry, I'm just extra stressed right now. We've never done this before."

"It's okay, I get it," Katie replied.

"If you need anything, just let me know, okay?" I asked.

Katie started shooing me away. "Of course, now go, scoot. Enjoy the show."

I chuckled. "I'm going, I'm going. See you in a bit."

I think I was overdue for a cup of coffee. Maybe that would help settle my nerves. Half a cup later, I was feeling better. Returning to the Cupid room, I caught the tail end of Fannie's show. She was so creative. The things she could do with Fannie were amazing.

Brides were busy walking around. The room was filled with happy brides and their friends and family, talking and laughing. Moving on, I headed into the Heart room. Chelsea had quite a crowd at our booth. Hopefully, we'll drum up some new business.

"Leah?" a voice called out from behind me.

I turned around and Sally approached me.

"What's up?" I asked.

"There's something you must see up front," she replied.

"Okay." I followed her to the front.

When we arrived up front, no one else was around except Meg who was still positioned at the table.

"I'm confused," I said looking over at Sally.

"It's outside. Come over here, I'll show you," Sally said gesturing at me to follow her towards one of our front windows. She pulled back one of the shears.

I gasped. In the front of our building, a woman holding a

sign marched back and forth. "Who is that?"

Sally shrugged. "No idea. She doesn't look familiar to you?"

I squinted while trying to read the woman's sign. "Not at all."

I had to wait until she turned back and faced the building again. Finally, I could read it. It stated, 'Save Your Money' on the top. In the middle was a picture of a wedding dress with a big red circle around it and a slash mark through the circle. At the bottom, it stated, 'Boycott Grand Lush'.

People were still arriving at the bridal show. This was not good. My heart began racing and sweat started to bead on my forehead. I paced, wringing my hands while trying to decide what to do. I needed to stop whatever was going on and fast. I asked Sally and Meg to remain inside, while I headed out to diffuse the situation.

I approached the woman. "Excuse me. Ma'am, what are you doing?"

About average height, with long blonde hair, and green eyes, she appeared to be in her mid to late twenties. The woman looked kept and clean, and no signs of anything odd stuck out. Except that she was holding a one-woman protest in front of my business.

"I'm letting everyone know not to shop at that horrible excuse for a bridal shop, Grand Lush Bridal Salon. The number one place for your number one day my arse. They are nothing but liars, and people need to know!" she exclaimed.

Whew! She was peeved. I cleared my throat. "Miss…I'm sorry what's your name?" I inquired.

"Tori. Tori Matthews," she replied.

"Ms. Mathews, I'm not sure what happened, but you need to take it up with the company," I explained.

"What happened is that they ruined my wedding dress two weeks before my big day and refused to refund my money or replace my dress. I sent it in for alterations and it was all messed up," Ms. Matthews said through gritted teeth.

"I'm very sorry to hear that. Have you filed a complaint with the Better Business Bureau?" I questioned.

"I did, but nothing came of it," she replied.

"Again, I'm very sorry but I must ask that you remove yourself from the property and handle this through the proper channels. This is private property, and we have an event going on," I pleaded.

"No one will listen! How else can I warn others?" she exclaimed.

Before I could come up with a response, a police cruiser had pulled up. The driver's side window rolled down. It was Luke Strickland, Meg's brother. He was an officer with the Ashford Police Department.

"Everything okay Leah?" he asked.

"I think so. I was telling Ms. Matthews here that she needed to leave because this was private property," I responded.

"No! I need to get the word out. They will ruin more bridal dresses, and nothing will be done!" she screeched.

"Leah, why don't you go inside and let me talk to her." Luke advised. "I'll be sure she will no longer be a problem."

"Thank you, I appreciate it," I said before heading back inside.

CHAPTER FOUR

When I returned inside, Sally was waiting in front of her desk.

"What happened? Why is she here? What did she say?" she pelted me with questions.

"Okay, slow down. She had a bad experience at Grand Lush Bridal Salon and felt like protesting here was a good way to get attention," I explained.

Her face dropped. "Oh my, that's too bad."

"Did you call the police?" I asked.

She shook her head no. "I didn't, Meg called. Who knows what she was going to try, and we didn't want you to get hurt."

"I figured Luke could help diffuse the situation. Luckily, he was in the area. Didn't want to make a big deal out of it and file a report, etc.," Meg clarified.

I looked over at them. "Thank you, I appreciate it. I'm pretty sure she is harmless, but you can't be too careful. If she shows up again, will you let me know?"

"Of course," Sally replied.

I checked my watch. It was almost time for our demonstration. Heading back to the Cupid room, I went backstage. Katie was putting the different items in order.

"All set?" I asked.

"Yep. I figured you could go first and say a few words about the Wedded Bliss and our facilities. Then I can start the PowerPoint and finish with the visual examples," she explained.

"Perfect," I responded.

Thirty minutes later, our demonstration was done. The audience appeared very receptive to the various décor ideas. Especially the pictures of the decorated gazebo and garden areas. The final few hours of the show were uneventful. Meg, Chelsea, and I were tired, but it was a good tired.

The next morning came, and it was nice not to rush around. I left my bed and headed to the kitchen. I poured a cup of coffee and pulled out a bagel and cream cheese from the fridge. I sat at my kitchen table, split the bagel, and lathered both halves with cream cheese.

I picked up my cell phone and scrolled through the Wedded Bliss social media accounts. To my surprise, several people were already posting pictures and comments about the show. It was so cool to see people enjoy themselves. Once I finished, I set my dishes in the sink and headed back to my room to get dressed.

After I made the final touches, I left the house and drove towards the Wedded Bliss. My mind was going over the show so far and I hoped the last day would be uneventful and the protestor wouldn't be back. Entering the parking lot, there was no sign of her thankfully. Inside, Sally, Chelsea and Meg were standing around the front table.

"Morning ladies!" I exclaimed.

"Morning Leah!" Meg replied.

"Hey Leah!" Chelsea said.

"Everything going okay so far?" I asked.

"Yes. Chelsea and I were talking about how happy we are with the show especially being our first go at it," Meg said.

Chelsea nodded in agreement. "Plus, we're making a nice profit. Maybe we can consider making this an annual event. I'll crunch the numbers after today, but we should have some money to start some of the updates we've been thinking about."

"Really? That's fantastic news. Let's finish today strong, then we can meet up later. We'll do a review, look at the different aspects, what worked, what didn't work, and any changes we'd like to make for next time," I replied.

Meg and Chelsea nodded in agreement. "Sounds good," they said.

"Perfect. I'm going to stop by my office quickly before the doors open. I'll check in with you guys later."

The show was in full swing. Alastair Tuxedos started the first show on the stage. The owner, Nora Berry, chose a good mix of traditional, modern, and unique tuxedos. Bonnie from Bonnie's Cakery, took the stage next displaying traditional and non-traditional wedding cakes. Who knew donut cakes were a trend these days?

I walked over to Morris Videography's booth. Tim attended high school with Chelsea, Meg, and I. When we were younger, he always had a camera in his hand capturing every moment. So it's no surprise he ended up starting his own videography company.

"Hey, Tim. How's it going?" I asked.

"Hey Leah, pretty good," Tim responded.

"I just wanted to say thank you for coming. I hope you've

enjoyed the show."

"Of course. I appreciate the invitation. It's been good. I've met some nice brides and did some networking with several of the other vendors," he said.

"That's great. I'm glad to hear that," I replied.

"Did you hear they've started planning our ten-year reunion?" Tim asked.

"No, I hadn't."

"Yeah. Yesterday, Rachel Pratt was here with her bridesmaids checking out the show and she mentioned it. I offered her my services and I also told her she should stop and talk to you about holding it here," Tim said.

Inwardly, I groaned a little. Rachel Pratt was the head cheerleader and bane of my high school existence. She and her little friends, "All-that's", harassed Meg, Chelsea, and I all through high school. The worst incident was during our junior year. It was homecoming, and Meg, Chelsea, and I were at the mall looking for dresses. When we were outside the dressing room looking at ourselves in the big trifold mirror, Rachel distracted us, while two of her little minions stole our clothes from the dressing room. We had to stay in dresses until our parents arrived with new outfits. By the next morning, the word spread, and our bras and underwear were flying on the flagpole in the quad. However, business was business and could be a new avenue to follow.

I forced a smile. "You didn't have to do that, I appreciate it."

"Of course. We small business owners must look out for each other." Tim said smiling.

We said our goodbyes and I headed down the hall. Before I reached the Heart room, someone was calling my name. I turned around and saw Annie Price, Vanessa's assistant.

"Excuse me, Ms. Jordan?" Annie asked.

"You can call me Leah, what can I help you with?"

She looked rattled or nervous. Annie was twisting her hands together in front of her. "It's my boss. She's...she's...missing!" Annie whispered.

"You'll have to talk a little louder. I didn't quite catch what you said," I replied.

"Va-Vanessa, she isn't here. She's missing!" Annie said choking back tears.

I raised my eyebrows. "What do you mean missing?"

"I've tried her c-ell, and her home ph-phone...no answer," Annie stuttered as she wiped away tears.

I reached out and squeezed her hand. "Maybe, she's just overslept. When's the last time you talked to her? Did you talk to her after the show ended yesterday?"

"Yes. She told me she was going out for the night. That was the last I've heard from her," Annie explained between tears.

I hated seeing someone cry. "How about I see if the police will do a wellness check? They will stop by her place and just make sure everything's okay, and it will put your mind at ease."

She sniffled. "Really? They would? That would be great. Oh, thank you so much!"

I felt awful for her. "Can you handle the bridal fashion show, or should we cancel it?" I asked.

"Vanessa would be so mad if we canceled it." She shook her head. "I think I can handle it. I can get a couple of people from the store to help."

"People would understand," I reassured her.

"I'm sure Ms. Jordan, er Leah. Vanessa trusts me to make sure things go right and I don't want to disappoint her. Maybe she'll show up right?"

"I'm sure she will. I'll let you know when I hear from the police. Easier said than done, but don't worry, I'm sure she just had too much fun last night and slept in," I answered.

"Thank you, I appreciate your help. I'm going to finish getting ready and reach out to some of the employees," Annie said before scurrying off.

As much as I had hoped there weren't going to be any issues, I spoke too soon. Heading to my office, I closed the door behind me. Sitting down at my desk, I pulled out my cell phone and dialed the non-emergency number for the police department.

"Ashford Police Department non-emergency number. How may I direct your call?" the receptionist answered.

"Good afternoon, my name is Leah Jordan. I was calling to request a wellness check on someone," I explained.

"Please hold, let me transfer you to the patrol division," the receptionist directed.

The awful, canned music came over the line, cutting out every few words. After two songs, someone finally picked up.

"Officer Greer, patrol division, how can I help you?" he asked.

"Good afternoon, my name is Leah Jordan. I'm the owner of The Wedded Bliss and we are currently holding an event. One of our vendors has not shown up and we cannot get ahold of them. Would it be possible to have a wellness check on her?" I asked.

"Do you have the person's name and address ma'am?" the officer asked.

"Yes, it's Vanessa Mitchell. Let me pull up her address," I replied.

"Take your time ma'am," the officer said.

I wiggled my mouse waiting for my desktop to appear. Opening the bridal show folder, I clicked on the document for the vendor information.

"Here it is. Her address is 7914 Brandon Court," I said.

"Do you know what type of residence this is? Any special instructions or codes needed to enter the neighborhood or complex?" Officer Greer asked.

"A condo. Not that I am aware of, sir," I responded.

"We can have someone come out there within the next twenty to thirty minutes. They will be in contact once they're done," the officer advised.

"Let me give you my cell number, 555-1724," I said.

"Got it. One of our officers should be in touch soon," Officer Greer replied.

"Thank you, I appreciate it," I said hanging up.

Checking my watch, it was about time for the fashion show to begin. I decided to give Annie an update and make sure she was set for the show. When I reached backstage, it was as if I was looking at a different Annie. She was organizing people to line up, checking last looks Nothing like the meek, mild girl I met a couple of days ago.

"Hey, Annie, I just wanted to stop by and see if you were, okay?" I asked.

She glanced over at me. "Hey, Leah. Yes, things are going well. Thank you."

"Do you have a few seconds? Then I'll be out of your way." I asked.

"Sure," she responded as she finished fixing a dress.

I stepped over to the corner out of the way. "I just wanted to let you know I spoke with the police. They are going over to Vanessa's and perform a wellness check. Once, I hear something, I will let you know."

"Oh, thank you! That makes me feel so much better. I appreciate it," she responded.

"I better let you get back. I'll talk to you later, have a good show," I said.

"Thank you," Annie replied before she returned to the models.

I made rounds between the rooms, while also continually checking my phone and the time. It'd been almost an hour since I contacted the police department. No one has called. Maybe they called the Wedded Bliss line instead. Heading up to the front, I decided to check in with Sally.

"Sally, have we had any calls recently?" I asked.

"Hey Leah, not really. It's been quiet. A few people called to double-check the times for the show today and a telemarketer, why do you ask?" Sally replied.

"Oh, nothing. I was waiting for a callback. I gave them my cell number, but I thought maybe they called back on the office line instead," I explained.

She shook her head. "Nope, sorry. I can let you know if a call comes..."

Before Sally could finish her sentence, two police officers entered the front door.

"Oh no, not again," I murmured. The hair on my arms stood on end and a bad feeling settled in the pit of my stomach. Sally was visibly shaking. I reached out and squeezed her hand. "They must have found something pretty awful."

chapter five

"Good afternoon Ms. Jordan. Could we have a minute please?" the first officer asked.

Meg, Sally, and I all looked at each other.

"Sure. Why don't you follow me to my office," I suggested.

"After you, ma'am." Officer Daniels his name tag read.

I walked them to my office, shut the door behind us, and sat at my desk. "Please, gentleman, have a seat. How can I help you?" I asked.

"This is regarding the wellness check you contacted us about earlier today," Officer Daniels replied.

A feeling of dread took over my body. "They told me someone would call me back when they were done. Is everything okay? Did you talk to her?" I asked.

"Normally, we would have called, but this news isn't something that could be delivered over the phone," Officer Stanton, the second officer, added.

That didn't sound ominous or anything. "Oh. What's hap-pened?"

"We found Ms. Mitchell deceased at her residence," Officer Daniels stated.

I gasped covering my mouth. "Wait, what? How can that be?" I exclaimed.

"I'm sorry, but it appears Ms. Mitchell has met with foul play," Officer Daniels said.

"Oh my gosh, her assistant is going to be devastated. She's the one who realized she was missing," I replied.

"Is she here right now? We'd like to speak to her," Officer Stanton said.

"Yes. Let me have one of my associates bring her to the office," I replied.

Picking up my desk phone, I dialed the front desk and asked Sally if she would locate and bring Annie to my office. Sally started asking questions, but I told her I would have to fill her in later. A few minutes later, there was a knock on my office door. I opened it, thanking Sally while ushering Annie in and closing the door.

"Annie, thanks for coming. These officers need to speak to you for a few minutes regarding Vanessa. I'll step out and give you privacy. If you need anything, please let me know," I advised.

"Thank you", Officer Daniels replied.

Letting myself out of the office, I closed the door quietly. Turning left, I almost ran into Sally, pacing in the hallway.

I grabbed my chest. "Oh my gosh! You scared the crap out of me."

Her face fell. "Sorry, I was worried. What's going on?"

"Bad news, I'm afraid. Let's get Meg and Chelsea and then I'll explain what I know so far, so I don't have to repeat myself," I explained.

"Sounds good," Sally said.

Checking my watch, we still had a few hours left of the show. We need to decide to finish it out as planned or stop it early. Sally went to get Meg, and I went to get Chelsea. Katie was still here, so our booth was covered. Once we arrived at the conference room, we all took a seat.

"Are you going to keep us in suspense?" Chelsea asked.

I held my hand up. "No. I wanted to gather you all here because earlier the assistant from Grand Lush Bridal Salon came to me concerned because she had not heard from her boss. I called the police department and asked them to do a wellness check. Unfortunately, when they got to her home, they found her deceased."

The room grew silent.

"That's awful!" Sally exclaimed.

"Oh no, not again," Meg murmured.

"Do they know what happened?" Chelsea asked.

"They haven't told me any details. Annie her assistant is in my office right now talking to the police," I replied.

"What do we do?" Meg asked.

That's a good question. I wanted to get everyone else's input. "We need to decide what we want to do as a team. Should we end the show early or follow through with the remainder?"

Chelsea shrugged. "What do we even tell them?"

"Maybe we can say there is a water leak?" Meg suggested.

Sally nodded. "That could work."

"On the other hand, the vendors have all paid quite a bit to participate and there's only a few hours left. Also, they will still need time to tear down," I said.

"I don't think we should tell everyone. We don't want to create a panic," Meg reasoned.

"The show must go on," Chelsea said.

"Let's go back to our posts. I'll wait to see what happens with the officers. If anything, else comes up, let me know immediately," I instructed.

"Sounds good," they agreed.

When we came out, my office door was still closed. I decided to walk through the rooms, and everything was well. No one appeared to be aware anything was amiss. After the third room's loop concluded, I decided to wait in the hallway. A few minutes later, the officers and Annie exited.

"Ms. Price, here's one of our cards. If you think of anything, please, contact us. We'll be in touch," Officer Daniels instructed.

Annie nodded and took the card. "Yes sir, thank you."

Officer Daniels' gaze turned towards me. "Ms. Jordan, could we have a few minutes of your time?"

"Of course." I turned to look at Annie. "Will you be okay to finish the rest of the show?"

"I'm going to do my best," Annie said before she walked down the hall.

I ushered them back into my office. "Officers, please come have a seat."

"Thank you," they responded.

"What else can I help you with?" I asked.

"We'll need a list of all your vendors, staff, and their contact information," Officer Daniels instructed.

"We can prepare that for you. It may take me a couple of days," I replied.

"That's fine. As soon as you can get it to us, we would appreciate it," Officer Stanton said.

"Is there anything else?" I asked.

"Not at this time. Ms. Price gave us information and some possible leads to get started. Here is my card. Call me when that list is ready. Also, we may need to call you and your staff in for questioning, as the case develops," Officer Daniels said.

I took the card from him. "Of course."

"Thank you for letting us use your office," Officer Stanton said.

"You're welcome," I said.

The rest of the show went off without a hitch. Meg and Sally left at the end, while Chelsea and I stayed behind. We wanted to make sure the vendors got torn down and packed up. Once everyone left, we met in my office.

"What a day," Chelsea said plopping down in one of my chairs across from my desk.

I let out a deep sigh. "That's an understatement. Not how I wanted the show to end,"

"No. Overall, look at the show, it was a success. I lost count of how many happy brides were here. I need to recalculate the ticket sales, but we did well," Chelsea said.

"Good. We couldn't have asked for a better turnout, especially for our first time. Several vendors I spoke with were having a great time and enjoyed the show," I smiled.

"Then I would call it a success." Chelsea half-heartedly pumped her fist into the air.

I shook my head. "Despite the info we got about Ms. Mitchell. I can't believe it. Why would someone do such an awful thing? Two murders in Ashford in less than six months, this isn't normal," I murmured.

"I know, it's awful. I don't think we'll ever know why people commit such heinous crimes. We will cooperate with whatever the police department needs and hope they find the culprit, so her family gets justice," Chelsea replied.

"I hope so. Let's lock up and get out of here," I replied.

Chelsea and I walked out together and said our final good-byes. Due to current circumstances, I decided to close the Wedded Bliss and give everyone Monday off. We were all exhausted from the busy weekend and emotionally and mentally drained.

By lunchtime Tuesday, the staff was already halfway done tearing down from the bridal show. It was business as usual. I spent the first part of my morning gathering the completed passports for the grand prize drawing so we could notify the winner. Then I began compiling the list of employees and vendor information the police requested.

Meg stuck her head in. "Hey, I was going to head out and grab some lunch, would you like anything?"

"Yes, I'm starving! That would be great. Where are you going?" I asked.

"I thought I would just go to Gibson's Deli," Meg replied.

"Sounds good. I'll take a chicken salad sandwich on wheat bread with lettuce and onion and a bag of kettle potato chips. Thank you," I said.

"Got it. Be back in a bit," Meg said as she headed out.

The list ended up being longer than I thought at about two and a half pages. I looked over it and checked for any errors. Finishing my sandwich, I printed two copies, one for our records. Grabbing a folder from the bottom left drawer, I slid the list in and headed out.

I found a parking spot in front of one of the parking meters. I placed enough coins in for the time limit, grabbed my folder, and went inside. The front area was very dreary, poorly lit, and empty. Several black banquet chairs sat around the perimeter of the room. In the front was the main desk, and in the right corner was a walled-off office area with a double-paned sliding window.

Walking up to the window, I noticed a sign posted. It said, 'Ring bell for service'. To the right, on the wall, was a small doorbell. I pushed it and nothing happened. Just as I was going to push it again, the glass window slid open, and an older gentleman peered out.

He cleared his throat. "Welcome to the Ashford Police Department. How can I help you?"

"Good afternoon, I'm here to see Officer Grover please," I answered.

"May I have your name please?" he asked.

"Leah Jordan," I replied.

"All right, ma'am. Let me check and see if he is available." The gentleman picked up his phone, briefly conversed, and hung up. "Ma'am, if you have a seat, Officer Grover will be out to see you in just a few minutes," the gentleman instructed.

"Thank you," I replied, crossing the room and sitting in one of the black chairs across from the office.

A bit later, Officer Grover stepped out from the door to the left of the office and asked me to follow him back. The last time I'd been past the door before a few months ago was probably a field trip back in the fourth grade. We turned down a hall on the left and he led me into an empty integration room.

"Please take a seat, Ms. Jordan," Officer Grover directed.

Once I sat down, he shut the door and joined me at the table.

"I wanted to drop off the list you needed us to compile that we discussed," I said, pulling it out of the folder and handing it over.

"Great. I appreciate your diligence," he replied.

He took a few minutes to review the list. I sat quietly until he finished. The silence was deafening.

I cleared my throat. "Is there anything else you need?"

"This looks fine. If you have a few minutes, I wouldn't mind asking you a few questions since you're already here," Officer Grover responded.

"I don't think that would be a problem," I said.

"Great. Let me grab my notebook and file. Would you care for a cup of coffee while you wait?" he offered.

I smiled. "That would be nice, thank you."

Once he left the room, I grabbed my cell and quickly called Sally to let her know I might be back later than I originally planned. After placing my phone back in my pocket, Officer Grover returned with two coffees and sat them down.

"Here you go," he said handing me a tan paper coffee cup with a white lid. "I didn't know how you took your coffee, so I brought cream and sugar packets." He pulled them from his pocket and placed them on the table in front of me.

"Thank you," I said grabbing a creamer and a couple packets of sugar.

"Now let's get started with the interview. You understand you are here under your own free will, and providing a statement at this time," Officer Grover advised.

"Yes, I do," I replied.

"First can you tell me how you know the victim, Vanessa

Mitchell?" he asked.

"Ms. Mitchell was a vendor at a bridal show my company, The Wedded Bliss, was holding over this past weekend," I responded.

He scribbled in his notebook. "How long have you known Ms. Mitchell?"

"I would guess approximately six weeks give or take. We first met her when we began planning for the bridal show. One of our former clients recommended her as a vendor," I explained.

"How would you describe Ms. Mitchell?" Officer Grover asked.

"In the brief time I got to know her, she was a savvy businesswoman, but a little shrewd at times. At first, she seemed pleasant enough, but once we met in person, she didn't come off as such a nice person," I replied.

His head snapped up. "How so?"

I shrugged. "I guess kind of snotty, 'I'm better than you' kind of vibe?"

"We understand an altercation occurred between Ms. Mitchell and a fellow vendor. What can you tell me about that?"

"Yes, it wasn't a big deal, just a disagreement regarding spacing. We came to a compromise and then everything was fine. I just chalked it up to being stressed about setup and the show," I replied.

He scribbled furiously. "Did you observe her interact with any of her employees?"

"The only one I met was Annie Price, her assistant. Ms. Mitchell was a little hard on her, but Ms. Price never spoke a bad word against her boss. Annie was very concerned and upset when she asked me to help find Ms. Mitchell."

"Is there anything else you can think of that may be pertinent to our investigation?" Officer Grover asked.

"There was a minor issue on Saturday. We handled it without any further issues," I said.

That caught his attention. "Can you provide me some more details please?"

"A woman was holding a one-person protest outside of our building. She was a former client of the Grand Lush Bridal Salon and was unhappy with her service. She wanted to express her freedom of speech," I explained.

"Do you happen to know her name?" he inquired.

"Tori Matthews. She was asked to leave, and we never saw her again."

"Can you describe her to me?"

"She was in her mid to late twenties, blonde hair, green eyes, about average height."

The officer finished writing in his notebook and closed it shut. "I think that's enough for now. Thank you for your time, Ms. Jordan, and for the list. If we need anything else, we'll be in touch."

"Of course." I stood up and shook his hand. He escorted me back to the front. From what I could gather, they had already talked to some people if they were aware of the altercation between Vanessa and Fannie. I got in my car and headed back to the office.

CHAPTER SIX

Barely settled back in my office, Sally appeared at my door. "Leah, do you have a minute?"

Looking up, I could tell that something was weighing on her mind. Sally's face was tense, and her brows furrowed. "Of course, what's up?" I asked.

She took a seat. "I just got off the phone with Theresa Sutter, my friend from church. The cops took Fannie in for questioning and have also searched her home and business."

I sat up straighter in my chair. "Wait, what?"

"Rumor has it, Vanessa may have been poisoned, and they think it was from a plant-like substance or flower. Who else could that point to?" Sally crossed her arms and began lightly shaking her head in disbelief. "It can't be her, can it?"

I shook my head. "No way. Fannie is one of the sweetest, most caring people I know."

"Exactly!" she exclaimed. "Theresa told me she heard if Fannie gets arrested and charged, she's going to have to use her business as collateral for her bond and she could end up losing everything."

"That's awful," I replied.

"Which is why I have been wanting to talk to you. I know we have a lot going on here, but Fannie could *really* use your help. Like you did a few months ago," she pleaded.

Not long after I took over The Wedded Bliss, we were hired to hold the wedding of a young socialite. It was a big coup. The income we earned would help keep our doors open. The night of the rehearsal, I found the groom-to-be dead in the basement of The Wedded Bliss. Chelsea, my best friend, became the number one suspect and was arrested. I soon found myself jumping in headfirst trying to find the real killer. With help from a private investigator Caleb, and Meg's older brother Luke, we cleared Chelsea's name and found the real killer.

I held my hands up and shook them. "Oh, I don't know. I'm not a professional. I was trying to help one of my best friends and our business. It was a fluke. Plus, I almost got hurt, er killed."

Sally looked down her glasses at me. "She's practically family, though. Fannie and your aunt were very good friends. She is widowed and doesn't have any of her own family. It made them kindred spirits. I'm sure she would be in your debt for any help you could offer."

She had to play the aunt card. Sally was not only smart, but she knew my weaknesses. I owed everything to my aunt for stepping in and raising me after my parents died. I wouldn't be half the woman I was today without Aunt Sissy's love and support.

I sighed. "You had to go there. I could do a little snooping I guess."

Sally clasped her hands together in joy. "Oh, thank you!"

I held my finger up. "Now, hold on. I'm not promising anything, but I will do my best."

"Thank you! Thank you!" Sally exclaimed, jumping up and running around my desk to hug me.

"Okay, okay. You're squeezing me too tight!" I managed to squeak out.

Sally jumped back. "Sorry!"

"It's okay," I said.

"If I can help with anything, please let me know," Sally said before heading out the door.

"I will."

I left work at the end of the day and decided to wait until I got home to start thinking about Vanessa and Fannie. Heading right to the kitchen, I opened the fridge to check my options. Nothing looked appealing, so I ordered pizza. After it arrived, I curled up in my recliner with a notebook. The list I compiled would give me plenty of people to talk to, but I really needed to start by learning more about Vanessa.

The cats must have smelled the pizza and finally woke from their hibernation. Oreo led the charge jumping up on the arm of the recliner and trying to pilfer a pepperoni. Her sister Patches was not far behind.

"Excuse me missy? That's my pizza. I know there's food in your bowls," I admonished her.

"Meow, me-owwwww," Oreo responded giving me the most pitiful look.

"Fine, twist my arm." I made her get down, then pulled off a few pepperonis and some cheese. I split the pieces in half and laid down a little pile for her and her sister.

Grabbing my laptop from the end table, I turned it on. Once it booted up, I clicked on the browser. Inputting Vanessa's name, I hit search and got a gazillion results. Great. Moving the mouse back to the search bar, I added Grand Lush Bridal Salon and Ohio. Perfect.

One of the first results was a link to her Instagram. It was full of selfie after selfie. Finally, I found a picture of a gentleman at a very nice restaurant. The caption read, 'Out with my love' and it was posted a few weeks ago. Luckily, she tagged him in the photo, his name was Hoyt Walker. One new lead already.

Facebook was a lot of the same, selfies. Moving to the About Me section, it listed that she was previously an employee at Vivian Ricci Designs in New York City. What was a designer from New York City doing in a small little town like Ashford? Going back to the search results, I scrolled down and found a link to an article about the Grand Lush Bridal Salon's grand opening.

Written four years ago in the Columbus Dispatch, it was a local girl done well story. Vanessa Horowitz, as she was known back then, was coming back to town to open her very own bridal store. In the story, Vanessa was quoted as 'Wanting to bring high-end fashion to the brides of small-town Ohio'. The rest of the article discussed the designer's experience, and that they would carry Vanessa's exclusive line H.E.A. Bridal, along with other top-line designers, and concluded with details about the grand opening itself.

Skimming the other results, there wasn't anything else of note. It wasn't until I got to the bottom of the list of results and there was a link to a website called Buyers B-ware. Once I clicked the link, it took me to a message board where consumers could post reviews of businesses for others to be aware of or avoid altogether. The only negative review the Grand

Lush Bridal Salon had was written by none other than Tori Matthews.

I added her name to the list of people to talk to. She had it out for Vanessa. Clearing the search bar, I typed in Vanessa Horowitz. In the results, an alumni website from Barton High School was listed. The site appeared to be run by alumni and not affiliated with the school.

Scrolling down, someone posted pictures from their year-books. I decided to start in 2003, give or take a few years. Nothing in 2003, or 2004. I pulled up the section for 2005 and began searching alphabetically. Finally, I reached the 'H"s.

My eyes must have been deceiving me. The picture of Vanessa Horowitz looked nothing like Vanessa Mitchell I had met a few days ago. Vanessa Horowitz was plain, with long dark hair, dark-rimmed glasses, a blue sweater set, and braces.

To say she'd had work done, was an understatement. Under her picture, it listed all her activities: Math Club, Newspaper, and Choir. I scrolled further down the page to see if there was anything else that might be pertinent. There were more pictures and one in particular caught my eye. It was none other than Annie Price. She looked the same, just younger. I made a note to ask her about her relationship with Vanessa.

By the time I finished, it was getting late, and I was exhaust-ed. Closing my laptop and setting it aside, I gathered my dishes, notebook, and folder. Heading towards the kitchen, I laid my folder and notebook by my purse. I called the kitties to follow, it was time for bed.

Sleep didn't come easy. I woke up several times throughout the night thinking about the past few days and helping Fannie. It was bittersweet, we had one of the biggest events of the year since I took over, but another tragedy occurred. Ashford has always been so quiet and peaceful and now two murders in less than six months. It was a little unsettling.

After tossing and turning some more, I finally threw the covers off, stood up, and shuffled out to the kitchen. Checking the clock on the microwave, it read 6:05 am. Pouring myself a cup of coffee, I sat on my back deck. Soaking in the quiet, I tried to relax and wake up. By the time my cup was empty, I felt a lot better.

I headed inside, set my cup in the sink, and put out fresh water and food for the cats. When I walked to my room, I noticed them both sprawled out on the bed, fast asleep. Moving quietly, I took a quick shower and got dressed. Back in the living room, I grabbed my bags, then picked up a coffee and a blueberry muffin on the way.

"Morning Leah, how are you?" Sally greeted me as I walked into the office.

I let out a sigh. "I'm okay. Didn't sleep too well last night."

A look of concern fell across her face. "Oh no. Are you getting sick?"

"No, just a lot on my mind," I replied before sipping my coffee.

Sally gestured with her head towards the hall. "Your 9 a.m. appointment is already in your office."

I was so confused. "My appointment?" I didn't realize there was one on my calendar?"

"Oh, maybe I forgot to tell you with all the hubbub going on." Sally's mouth turned into a frown. "Sorry."

I smiled. "It's okay, I'll check back in with you later."

Walking to my office, I tried racking my brain about this appointment. I knew there was one set up with a prospective couple, but I was sure that wasn't until tomorrow. Taking a deep breath, I opened my office door and walked inside.

"Good morning, I'm so sorry you've had to wait. Let me just put my stuff down and I'll be right with you," I said striding over to my desk.

"No need to rush Jordan," the male voice replied.

I almost dropped my coffee. Turning around, sitting across from my desk was Caleb Hamilton. He was a pleasant sight. His dark hair was gelled back except for a small piece that fell over his left eyebrow. He wore a form-fitting navy dress shirt with khakis and brown dress shoes. I got a whiff of his cologne and inwardly swooned.

"What are you doing here?" I exclaimed as I sat in my chair.

"A little birdie told me you might need help with another case you stumbled into." He crossed his arms behind his head and leaned back into the chair.

"Oh, is that so?" I raised my eyebrow. "Who is this little birdie of which you speak?" I already had a pretty good idea.

Caleb winked. "I can't reveal my source."

"Uh-huh. Sally has a big mouth."

We both laughed.

"Now, she's just worried about you and figured you could use some help. Admit it, we made a pretty good team last time," he said.

"We did, and you're right, she considers Meg, Chelsea, and I like her daughters. I can't fault her for caring. I thought you were busy working that surveillance case for that rich fancy client?" I asked.

"I did, and it's completed already. Turns out they were both cheating on each other," he explained.

"Oh my. Can't imagine that will end well," I murmured.

"Probably not, they will have to fight it out in court. I did my job," he replied.

"There's nothing else going on that requires your full attention?" I asked.

Caleb raised an eyebrow. "Why Jordan, are you trying to get rid of me already?"

My stomach fluttered a little. He was so sexy, even when he wasn't trying to be serious. We first met when I picked him up at the airport a few months ago and soon became partners in investigating the groom's death and clearing Chelsea's name. He was different than the guys I dated previously. He was so caring, sometimes frustrating, but he challenged me.

"No, not at all. I know you're usually in high demand."

"Not now. A few small jobs and background checks." He sat up in his chair. "Why don't you fill me in on what's going on here?" Caleb asked.

"We were having our bridal show. On the last day, one of our vendor's assistants approached me concerned because she thought her boss was missing. After asking her some questions, we decided to contact the police department to conduct a wellness check and when they went to check on her boss, they found the home broken into, and her boss murdered," I explained.

Caleb grew silent for a minute. "Did you know the victim very well?"

"Not really. Only since we began accepting vendors for the bridal show. She wasn't the most pleasant person. She reminded me a little bit of Janie Coleman with her better-than-thou attitude but more mature," I said.

"Wow, she sounds interesting. How can I help?" he asked.

"I haven't gotten that far yet actually. Last night, I started researching on Vanessa Mitchell and compiled a list of people to follow up with."

"Awesome Jordan. What did you learn so far?"

"She's a local girl from Barton who used to be a fashion designer in New York City. She came back to Ashford in 2011 and opened her bridal shop. Vanessa has a boyfriend named Hoyt Walker and she and her assistant Annie Price went to high school together," I replied handing him the notes I had taken thus far.

He skimmed them briefly. "What about potential suspects?"

I took the notes back. "I'm still adding to the list. Annie and Hoyt would be on automatically as they are the closest to her."

"Very good. What about Fannie? She's the police's primary suspect?" he asked.

"She is the sweetest person I know. There is no way she could have done this. I can't even believe the police would think she was guilty." I groaned.

"Right, we still need to talk to her, Jordan, and verify her alibi. Then we can eliminate her. Anyone else so far?"

"There was a woman, Tori Matthews who showed up here Saturday protesting that she had a bad experience with Vanessa and her bridal salon," I explained.

"Protesting? Whew! You've been busy. If you want, I can start researching some of these people and see what I find out," Caleb offered.

"That would be great. I thought I would pick up some pastries and visit Fannie to talk to her. Also, stop by Vanessa's to pay my condolences and see if I can find out more about the boyfriend," I said.

"Smart. Why don't we split up and reconvene and meet up later for dinner? My treat. I'll look further into Annie Price, the boyfriend, and the protestor," Caleb said.

"You're paying? How can I say no." I laughed.

"Great, I'm going to run a couple of errands and check into my hotel at the Ashford Inn." He stood up and began walking to the door. Then he turned around. "Jordan, be careful."

"Always, Hamilton." I winked.

Caleb made a face. "Mm-hmm."

CHAPTER SEVEN

O nce Caleb left, I shut down my computer and headed out. Driving to Bonnie's Bakery, I decided to grab some chocolate turnovers for Fannie and a variety of muffins to drop off at Vanessa's. Back in my car, I called the flower shop. After speaking to one of her employees, I found out she was at home.

I pulled my phone out and mapped the address. She lived in a cute little condo community for seniors. I parked several spots down, grabbed the box of turnovers, and walked up to her front door. I knocked.

She opened the door right away. "Leah? What are you doing here? Come in."

Fannie was short, with short curly brown hair and brown eyes. She was wearing gray straight-leg sweatpants and a light-yellow shirt. You could see bags under her eyes and her usual cheery demeanor was missing.

"I called the shop, and Priscilla informed me that you stayed home today," I replied.

She sighed. "I did. My arthritis is flaring up. Plus, the girls have it under control. Come in, have a seat."

I followed her into the living room. It was adorable. A floral blue couch sat along the wall to my left, a tan recliner at the end, and a coordinating blue high-back chair on the other wall next to the fireplace. The room led back to a small kitchen/dining room. She sat in the recliner next to the couch, and I sat on the end closest to her.

I placed the box of turnovers on the little coffee table. "Thank you for letting me stop by."

She smiled. "You didn't have to bring anything."

"I know, but Aunt Sissy always taught me it was good manners when you visit someone else's home," I replied.

"I take it you heard about the police interrogating me?" she asked.

Okay, I guess there is no beating around the bush. "How did you know?"

"One, you haven't been to my house since before you went to college, two, if my nose doesn't deceive me, those are Bonnie's famous chocolate turnovers. There are only two things they are good for, breakfast or drowning your sorrows. I figure it's the latter," she responded.

"Can't put anything past you. You're right, Sally told me she heard about them questioning you and that they now consider you a suspect. I wanted to see how you were doing and offer my help," I said.

"That is so sweet of you. I appreciate it. The past couple of days have been rough. I heard about what happened to that poor girl, but I had nothing to do with it. She and I may have had a conflict at the show, but I'm too old to hold grudges, let alone hurt another person," she elaborated.

She was being sincere. I could tell by watching her face. "I know that, and anyone else who knows you does too. Can you tell me what they said?"

"The police called me in for questioning, I didn't think anything of it. I had nothing to hide. Very quickly, I realized it was heading in a more serious direction when they started asking about the flowers I had at the bridal show and in my shop.," Fannie explained.

"Did they mention any specific ones?" I asked.

"Yes, a few. Callalily, Hydrangea, and Iris. But they are common flowers you can find at any floral store, nursery, or personal garden."

I wrote down the names of the plants to research later. "Do you have an alibi for the night of the murder?"

"I was here at home, alone. Not a solid one, I know. My assistant Priscilla and I went back to the shop after the show, stored the flowers and I locked up the shop. Came home, ate dinner, and relaxed watching television until I fell asleep in my recliner," she explained.

"No one can verify that?" I asked.

She shook her head. "I don't think so. My neighbor next door on the right, Nora is away visiting her grandchildren and Paul the one on the other side is hard of hearing and a hermit."

"I see. Do you know if anyone has security cameras?" I asked.

"I think we do, why?" she asked.

"If we can show that you didn't leave and your car was still here, then maybe it can help prove your alibi," I said.

"What about the poison? They claim it's from my shop!" she exclaimed.

I reached out and squeezed her hand. "I'll have to investigate that further. Let's not worry just yet."

"Is there anything else you want to know?" Fannie asked.

"Did you and Vanessa talk much during the bridal show?" I asked.

"Not really. I spoke to her assistant Annie more. I felt bad, Vanessa was harsh to her, always ordering her around," she answered.

"Did you notice Vanessa talk to anyone else besides other vendors or brides?" I asked.

"Now that you ask, a man stopped by her booth. He was alone and didn't appear to be with a bride or with a group. At one point, I saw Vanessa talking to him and then they walked away together," Fannie said.

"Were you able to hear anything? Or catch his name?" I asked.

"I'm sorry, I didn't. They were just far enough out of earshot," Fannie replied.

"That's okay. Could you describe him?"

"He was young, maybe early to mid-twenties, Hispanic looking and had a muscular build."

I wrote down the details. "Great I'm going to do some investigating and see if we can clear your name."

Fannie began to tear up. "I can't believe you're going to do that for me."

"Of course. You were one of my aunt's best friend and if she was here, I know she would want to help you too," I said.

She brushed away a couple of tears that had fallen down her cheeks, and grabbed my hand. "Thank you so much. I appreciate it."

"I don't want to take up too much of your time. I will start looking into some of these leads and see what I can find. In the meantime, give Lou Little a call. He's our attorney and it might be good to get some advice just in case," I suggested. "He and Aunt Sissy were friends too, and I am sure he would give you a free consultation."

"I'll reach out to him. Thank you again for your help,"

Fannie replied.

"Of course. If you think of anything else, please let me know," I instructed.

I pulled a card from my bag and handed it to Fannie. As she reached to take it, I squeezed her hand. "It will be okay.

Vanessa's house was not what I expected. It was a ranch home with a cute front porch decorated to the hilt for fall and looked like a page out of a home and garden magazine. Two cars sat in the driveway, so I parked on the street. Picking up the box of muffins from the passenger seat, I exited my car and walked up to the front door.

Before my fist connected to the door for a second knock, it flew open! Standing on the other side was Hoyt Walker. I recognized him from Vanessa's social media. He appeared to be in his early to mid-forties with short gray hair, and an average to husky build, he wore a blue dress shirt, tie, and khakis. In his left hand, he held a cell phone to his ear.

"No Charlie, I'll call you back. Someone's here. Just tell them we'll have to reschedule the conference call," he said hanging up.

"Good afternoon," I said.

"You're with the cleaning company, right? Thank God! They told me someone would be here over an hour ago," he grumbled.

"No sir. My name is Leah Jordan. I own The Wedded Bliss. I heard about what happened to Vanessa and wanted to pay my respects," I explained.

He stepped aside and gestured for me to enter. "Oh! I'm sorry. Things have been a little hectic around here. Please, come in. My name is Hoyt Walker. I am...er was Vanessa's fiancé."

"Thank you," I said stepping inside.

"Please excuse the mess. I just got back into town from a business trip and haven't had time to straighten up. The police just allowed me access to the house this morning," he said.

"No need to apologize. I'm so sorry for your loss Mr. Walker," I said as he led me into a living room just off the foyer.

"Thank you. I can't wrap my mind around it. I spoke with Vanessa Saturday night before I went to a business dinner, and everything was fine. The next thing I know, my secretary is blowing my phone up trying to get ahold of me to tell me...to tell me..." Mr. Walker's voice cracked.

The poor man. He seemed so broken.

I placed the box of muffins on the coffee table. "I know that it must be difficult right now. Is there anything I can do?"

"That's so nice of you to offer, but her assistant has offered to help me. How did you know Vanessa?" he asked.

"She was a vendor at a bridal show my company recently held," I replied.

"Oh yes. I remember now. Did Vanessa seem to be acting out of sorts or as if something were wrong?" he asked.

"Unfortunately, I didn't get to know her well, but I saw her over the weekend, she was happy talking to brides at her booth," I explained.

"That sounds like Vanessa. She always had a strong work ethic. That's one of the things that attracted me to her when we first met," he commented.

"How long had you two been together?" I asked.

"We dated for three years and got engaged six months ago. She had been putting in extra time with the bridal shop all while planning our wedding," he responded.

"Sounds like she had a full plate," I said.

"I tried to convince her to hire a wedding planner, but she would have none of it. I travel so much that I knew I wouldn't be able to help. She insisted she would be fine," he explained.

Tears began welling in his eyes.

"It's a bride thing. We want everything to be perfect on our special day," I said.

He wiped his eyes and cleared his throat. "Yeah, I can see that."

"I don't want to keep you, I just wanted to stop by, pay my

condolences, and drop off these muffins," I said.

"I appreciate it. I know Vanessa would also," he said.

Mr. Walker's cell phone rang. He pulled it out and looked at it.

"I'm sorry, I have to take this," he apologized.

I smiled. "No problem, I can show myself out." I got up and walked to the front door, closing it quietly behind me.

Just as I reached my car, a woman was jogging by. "Shame, what happened to that woman," she commented.

"Yes, a horrible tragedy," I replied.

"Are you a cop?" she asked.

"No, not a cop. But I am looking into what happened to Ms. Mitchell," I replied.

"I feel sorrier for the fiancé. Poor man never knew the minute he went out of town, she had her side piece over," she murmured.

I almost choked. Side piece? "I'm sorry, what did you say?"

"No one talked about it, but we all knew, she didn't hide it. Hoyt was too good for her. Hopefully, now he can find a good woman," she replied.

She seemed to know quite a bit. This was great information.

"Do you know the guy that Vanessa was seeing?" I asked.

"Not personally. He always showed up in one of those work pickup trucks. There was some type of plant or leaves on the side," the woman described.

My ears perked up. Plant? I made a mental note.

"Did you know Vanessa well then? Is there anyone you think would want to harm her?"

"I knew her, but I didn't *know* her. She was not the friendliest neighbor. She was always yelling at the kids in the neighborhood for playing too loud and interrupting her while she was working. What a piece of work! Who yells at kids for just having innocent fun?" the woman grumbled.

"Yeah, that's not very nice," I commented.

"As for who might have done it? I don't know. She certainly made more enemies than friends. You ought to talk to Mrs. DiCarlo across the street. She and Vanessa were always having issues," she said.

"I will. Thank you for talking to me. I didn't catch your name, I'm Leah Jordan," I said sticking out my hand.

"Missy, Missy Yates." She looked down at her watch. "I better get going, I need to pick up my son from school. Good luck. I hope they catch the killer."

"Thank you, me too," I replied.

Missy continued running off down the sidewalk. I headed to my car, and it took a few minutes to write down everything I had learned from Missy. I included the name of the neighbor across the street, Mrs. DiCarlo, making a note to follow up with her. Checking my watch, it was almost time to meet Caleb for dinner. After finishing my notes, I decided to head home to freshen up.

CHAPTER EIGHT

When I arrived home, Oreo and Patches were sprawled on the back of the couch in the front window snoozing. As soon as I opened the front door, they both jumped down and began rubbing up against my legs, purring and meowing.

"Hello girls, how are you?" I asked.

Sitting my bags on the hallway table, they followed me into the kitchen. I scooped food into their bowls and gave them fresh water before heading to my bedroom. Now for the question of the day, what to wear. I want to look nice, but not desperate. Finally, settling on a long gray cardigan over a long-sleeved mauve shirt I paired with jeans and brown boots.

I stepped into the bathroom to wash my face and brush my teeth. Applying lip gloss, I looked in the mirror and was satisfied. After I finished, the cats joined me in the bedroom, stuffed from dinner and splayed out on the bed.

I kissed each of them on their heads. "Keep the bed warm, girls. Mommy will be back in a couple of hours."

Stepping outside, a slight chill filled the air. Glad for my sweater choice, I pulled it close and hurried to get in my car. Thankfully, my heater warmed up quickly. By the time I arrived at the Ashford Inn, Caleb was already waiting outside. He entered on the front passenger side, slid in, and put on his seatbelt.

"Thanks for picking me up," he said.

I chuckled. "No problem. It's the least I could do since you're buying."

He laughed. "How'd your day go?"

"Actually, better than expected. How about yours?" I asked.

"Good, good. I have some information I think you'll find interesting," he replied.

"Same here. Let's wait till we get to the restaurant to discuss," I said.

"Agreed," he responded.

The rest of the ride was filled with general conversation. We arrived at Beckett's and the parking lot was full.

"Oh no," I murmured.

"They have valet. Why don't you have them park it?" Caleb asked.

"They charge too much. I'll drive around a few more times,

maybe someone will be leaving," I replied.

He let out a sigh. "Jordan don't be ridiculous. I'll pay. Just turn around and pull into the valet line."

"Fine, you win," I replied.

"I take it you don't visit Columbus much eh?" he asked.

I shrugged. "Not really."

"I'm sure it's like downtown Cleveland. Several restaurants, bars, and clubs have valets," he explained.

"You forget, this is Ashford. We're lucky to have more than three stoplights," I said.

"Touché," Caleb replied.

The valet arrived at the driver's side and opened my door. He waited until I stepped out, then tore off a ticket from a rearview mirror hanger and handed it to me.

"Ma'am, this is your claim ticket. Just bring it back up to the valet station when you leave and one of us will bring your car around. Enjoy your meals," he instructed.

"Thank you," I replied.

Caleb walked in front of me to hold the door open. "After you."

As soon as we stepped into Beckett's, the aromas in the air were incredible. Known for its filet and prime rib, it was the finest restaurant in Ashford, second only to Stella's. The hostess quickly found our reservation and seated us. The décor was sleek, with deep shades of burgundy, black, and silver.

I couldn't help but take it all in. Caleb must have noticed because he nudged me with his foot under the table.

"What?" I exclaimed.

He gestured at the gentleman standing to my right. "The waiter is here for our drink orders."

"Oh gosh! I am so sorry. I'll take water and a sprite please," I replied.

The waiter gave a curt nod. "Thank you, ma'am, and for you sir?' the waiter asked.

"I'll take an…" My date stopped mid-sentence and looked at me. "Are you okay if I have a beer?"

"Of course," I replied.

"Okay then, I'll take a Bud Light in a chilled glass please," Caleb said.

"Right away. I'll be back with your drinks and bread shortly. Look over your menus and let me know if you have any questions," the waiter said before leaving the table.

I began perusing the menu and my eyebrows immediately shot up. Holy crap! Twenty-five dollars for a six-ounce steak? The cow must have been fed organic. Looking at the sides, they were all over ten dollars. Caleb must have noticed the expression on my face.

He peered over his menu. "Anything looking good?"

"Oh, I haven't decided yet. Is there anything you recommend?" I asked.

"Their filet is top-notch, as well as their T-bone and prime rib. Great flavor and is always tender. As for sides, they have a nice side salad, cheesy au gratin potatoes, green beans with garlic and bits of bacon and their baked potatoes are huge," Caleb replied.

"Hmm, I think a small filet would be plenty. The salad and au gratin potatoes sound great as sides. If I have any steak leftover, the girls will be over the moon."

His eyebrows were raised. "They like steak, eh?"

"They do, I don't give it to them all the time. Just once in a blue moon," I explained.

"Gotcha," he replied.

Oh, man. I am sure the crazy cat lady neon sign was flashing above my head. "What are you getting?"

"I think I'm having a T-bone with a salad and baked potato. I'm starving. I didn't eat a lot today," he replied.

The waiter returned with our drinks, dropped off our bread as promised, and took our orders. Once he left, we got down to the investigation.

"Who wants to go first?" Caleb asked.

"You can go ahead," I said.

"Okay, let me pull out my notes," he replied. Caleb pulled out a notebook and flipped through a few pages.

"Who do you want to start with first?" I asked.

"Let's start with Tori Matthews. Her maiden name is

Charleston, age twenty-five, an Ashford resident. I checked for any arrest records, civil cases, etc. Nothing. I did find a couple of criminal trespassing charges. This girl has a thing for injustice. One of the charges stemmed from a protest last spring at a mini mart that sold expired food. The other last year at a sit-in protesting environmental causes at a factory," he rattled off.

"Wow, and to think I felt special she was protesting at our little bridal show," I replied.

"Sarcasm noted. Other than that, she's clean," he concluded.

"What about the boyfriend Hoyt Walker?" I asked.

"He's pretty boring. Forty-five, never been married, no kids, a senior vice president with an insurance company. Not even a parking ticket," Caleb replied.

"You may not think that when I tell you what I learned earlier," I commented.

"Oh? Do tell," Caleb said.

"Earlier, I stopped at Vanessa's residence and Mr. Walker was there. I brought some muffins and paid my condolences. He is very upset about what's happened and was very in love with Vanessa," I explained.

"That's not very titillating," Caleb replied.

"Wait, it gets better. When I left the house, that's when it got interesting. I ran into a neighbor, almost quite literally, and she had no problem telling me that Vanessa had been cheating on her fiancé. Mr. Walker of course didn't mention anything, but I don't think we can cross him off the list just yet. Jealousy makes a person do crazy things," I said.

"That it does. What else did you learn?" Caleb asked.

"A few things. First, I went to see Fannie. I had to see how she was holding up. She confirmed what Sally was told that the police had questioned her, and that Vanessa was poisoned. Also, from what it sounds like, the police are eyeing her as their number one suspect. They were very interested in the types of flowers and plants she stocks and had at the bridal show," I explained.

"Interesting..." Caleb said.

Before he could continue, the waiter arrived back at the table with our salads. We thanked him and waited until he left to continue.

"Where did we leave off?" I asked.

"You were talking about Fannie," Caleb replied.

"Right. Fannie also mentioned seeing a strange man talking to Vanessa at the bridal show. She couldn't give me a name, but did give me a description," I said.

"Great, I want to investigate that. Does she have an alibi?" he asked.

"She doesn't. Fannie said she stayed home all night. There may be cameras at her complex. We should check them out," I replied.

"Good idea. The last person I told you I would investigate was Annie Price, Vanessa's assistant. I found some interesting information. Did you know her father is none other than Sterling Walters?" Caleb asked.

I gasped. "You mean the politician with the goofy campaign ads, 'Win with Walters?'"

"Yep. The same. Annie is his only daughter, he also has three sons," he explained.

"Hmm, wonder why she goes by Price?"

"I figured you'd asked. Earlier in his career, there was a scandal between Walters and his communications director. They ended up having an affair and it didn't end well."

"Oh wow, go on," I urged.

"The communications director became pregnant, and Walters and Stella Price welcomed a baby girl," Caleb said.

"Wait, this from the same guy who's always touting family values?" I asked.

"The same. He is reformed now, has repented for his indiscretions, and even went through therapy. He's still married to his wife all these years later," Caleb explained.

"What a dark cloud to grow up under," I said.

He nodded. "Exactly my thought."

"What else did you find out?"

"Ms. Price has no criminal or civil records. She resides in an apartment, and she's worked for the salon since it opened," he added.

"I want to contact her and see what information she may have. As well as try and find this mystery side piece of Vanessa's. The neighbor told me I should speak to Mrs. DiCarlo, who lives across the street from Hoyt and Vanessa's," I said.

"I'm still waiting on financial records. One of my contacts is my go-to guy but he told me he's backed up now," he commented.

"Good idea. You don't happen to know anyone we could contact and find out more about the plants angle, do you?" I asked.

"I might, I'll check and let you know," Caleb replied.

The food was outstanding. The steak was so tender. It had such a great flavor and almost melted in your mouth. The potatoes, oh the potatoes, were so full of cheesy goodness. I felt like licking my fork, but I resisted.

We spent the rest of our meals just catching up and sharing stories. There were plenty of leftovers to take home and make the girls happy. Caleb paid the bill, and we headed out to the valet station.

"Thank you for dinner, it was amazing!" I exclaimed.

He grinned. "You're welcome. I'm glad you liked it. A friend recommended it to me the last time I was here, and I fell in love."

The valet greeted us as we approached the stand. "Good evening, did you two enjoy your meals?"

"Yes, thank you. Here's my ticket," I replied.

"We'll have your car up shortly ma'am," he instructed before he took off to retrieve the car.

It had cooled down quite a lot since we were inside, and I started to shiver. Caleb must have noticed. He took his jacket off and placed it on my shoulders. I thanked him and pulled the coat around me. His musky cologne wafted into my nostrils. Finally, the valet arrived with my car. Caleb handed him a tip and we headed out.

"What do you have going on tomorrow?" he asked.

"I have an appointment with a prospective bride and groom, but after that, I should be free," I replied.

"I have to search some court records for one of my clients, but I thought we could do some further investigating," he said.

"Sounds good." I pulled into the lot of the Ashford Inn. "Here we are," I said.

Caleb smiled. "Thanks for driving."

There it was, that smile. Suddenly my insides grew very warm, and it wasn't from the car heater. I liked him a lot and I think he liked me, but I didn't know if right now it was a good time to get into a relationship, especially a long-distance one. I also didn't want to ruin a good friendship.

"You're welcome," I replied.

Caleb leaned over to hug me and placed a kiss on my cheek. It felt like it was tingling.

"See you tomorrow Jordan," Caleb said as he exited the car.

I think I floated all the way home. The next thing I knew I was sitting in my driveway. A tapping sound pulled me out of the clouds. Looking to my left, someone was standing at my driver's side window. Holy crap! I cracked the window.

"Hello?" I called out.

The figure crouched down and when the light from my front porch hit them, I realized it was Luke Strickland. He wore his navy Ashford Police Department uniform and coat. His department ball cap covered his short blonde hair. He looked quite handsome except for the look of concern on his face.

I grabbed my chest. "You almost scared me to death! What are you doing here?"

"Sorry, I didn't mean to frighten you. I was patrolling the neighborhood and saw you sitting in your car in the driveway. Wanted to make sure you were all right," Luke apologized.

"You could have at least called out and identified yourself," I chided.

"I did. I called your name three times," he replied.

"Oh, sorry. I guess I was just zoned out," I said getting out of the car. Closing the door, I grabbed the key fob and hit the lock button.

"I'm glad you're okay," Luke replied.

He kept standing there like he wanted to say more.

"Did you want to come in?" I asked.

"Hmm...what? Oh, no, no, I shouldn't. I need to get back to my patrol," Luke said.

"Okay, have a good night," I said waving at him.

He began to walk back to his car, then turned around. "Leah?"

"Yes?" I asked.

"You're not going to get involved in the Mitchell investigation, are you?" Luke asked.

Who, me? "No, I think once was enough," I replied mentally crossing my fingers. I didn't have the heart to tell him I was already involved.

"Okay, good. Goodnight again Leah," Luke said.

"Goodnight," I said, heading inside my house.

I dropped my purse on the table and went to my room to change into pajamas. Settling in my recliner in the front room, I curled up with a fuzzy blanket and turned on the television. Just before the bride said yes to her dress, my cell rang.

"Hello?" I answered.

"Leah? It's Fannie. I'm so sorry to be calling you so late, but I remembered someone did see me Saturday night," she said.

"Really? That's great!" I exclaimed.

"After I got home the other night, I didn't feel like cooking and so I ordered a pizza from Tony's over on Elm. It arrived around nine-thirty," Fannie explained.

"Do you still have your receipt?" I asked.

"I do," Fannie replied.

"Great, I will call you tomorrow to get a copy of it," I said.

"Just let me know and I can stop by your office," Fannie responded.

"Sounds good. Have a good night," I said.

"Goodnight and thank you again, Leah," she said before she hung up.

A sense of relief came over me. Hopefully, I could confirm her order with Tony's and the police would agree Fannie was innocent. My first goal tomorrow though was talking to Annie and following up with Vanessa's neighbor - Mrs. DiCarlo.

CHAPTER NINE

"Thank you for meeting with us at the Wedded Bliss. We strive to provide you, your family, and your guests with a memorable experience for your special day. Why don't you tell me a little about you and your fiancé, Aubrey?" I asked.

"Thank you. This is Trent, my fiancé. We have been together for almost three years. We are huge fans of Beauty and the Beast. Trent and I met performing in the community theater production of Beauty and the Beast and you could say the rest is history," Aubrey explained as she rubbed his arm.

"That is so sweet. What time of year were you thinking about holding your ceremony?" I asked,

"Our favorite time of year is winter. So, we were thinking February," Aubrey replied.

Oh boy. That's only a few months away. "How many guests

were you planning on?"

"We want to keep it small and intimate. We've estimated seventy-five to one hundred guests," Trent spoke up.

"Do you have any thoughts on décor or a color theme yet?" I asked.

"We were thinking red, blue, gold and white. With evergreen accents and snow," Aubrey replied.

"That sounds beautiful. What were you thinking about as for your menu?"

"Since it was winter, we were thinking comfort type food. Chicken pot pies, beef tenderloin with potatoes and vegetables," Aubrey said.

"I think that would be a great menu. Let me show you, our packages. They can be tailored to meet your specific needs. Take them home, look over them and if you have any questions, please let me know," I said, handing over the packets. "Why don't we go tour our different room options and we can see which ones may work for your special day."

"Great, we'd love to," Aubrey replied.

"Just go ahead and follow me please," I instructed as I stood up.

Once they were ready, I led them down the hallway to the rooms.

"Our smallest room, the Love room is probably too small for the reception. However, if you chose to, you could use the

Love room for the ceremony and then transition to the Cupid room for the reception. I'll give you two some time to look around and consider the possibilities. When you're done, meet me at the doorway and we can move on," I directed.

"Thank you," Aubrey and Trent replied.

When they were ready, we moved on to the Cupid room.

"Now you'll have to use your imagination of course, but in the front, you can have the bridal table up on risers. The cake table could be placed in the front right corner. The dance floor could be in the middle in front of the bridal table and flanked by round tables and the food could be set up on the left side towards the front," I explained, gesturing as I spoke.

"What if we wanted to have a deejay?" Trent asked.

"I am sure that wouldn't be an issue," I responded.

Aubrey leaned over to Trent, whispering something in his ear. "I think we have a lot to talk about and process. We appreciate your time today. Trent and I want to take a couple of days to discuss everything. Then would it be okay if we follow up with you in a few days?"

"Of course. Look over everything and like I said, just let me know if you have any questions. I'll walk you out," I replied.

Once they were gone, I stopped at Sally's desk.

"Hey Leah, how did it go? They seemed sweet," Sally asked.

"Agreed. I think they'll book with us. They want a Beauty and the Beast-themed wedding in February," I replied.

"Ooh, that would be beautiful. I bet over at Taylor Transportation they have a sleigh they could rent. Wouldn't that be romantic with the snow?" Sally swooned.

"It definitely would," I agreed.

"How's it going with Fannie's case? Making any progress?" Sally asked.

"A little. I've been able to interview some people and do some research. I'll be able to cover a little more ground now that Caleb is in town. You wouldn't know how he heard about what was going on do you?" I asked.

"I'm sure he must have heard about it on the news," Sally replied keeping a straight face.

I raised an eyebrow and looked her right in the eye. "It hasn't been put on the news yet. You invited him, didn't you?"

Sally groaned. "Okay, you got me. I just figured some help would be good and you two made such a great team last time. Plus, you have to admit he's easy on the eyes." Sally fanned herself.

"Sally!" I exclaimed.

"What? I may be old, but I'm not dead yet," she replied with a shrug.

I laughed. "You are too much sometimes."

"That's why you love me." Sally winked.

"Anything going on?" I asked.

"Not too much, I talked to Chelsea earlier, and we've gotten a lot of new follows and likes on our social media pages," Sally replied.

"Hopefully those turn into calls and appointments," I said.

"I am sure they will. Don't worry, the bridal show was a rousing success," Sally said.

"It was, I just hoped we would be seeing a lot more results from it by now." I sighed.

"Be positive. The holidays will be here before you know it and there will be lots of engagements popping up and weddings," Sally said.

"I guess you're right. There are a few stops I need to make. Let me know if anything comes up," I said.

"Of course," Sally replied.

As I headed back to my office, I couldn't decide whether to stop and talk to Annie or follow up with Vanessa's neighbor. It would probably be best to see Annie first. I grabbed my bag and headed off to the bridal shop.

Located in uptown Ashford, the store was based in one of the homes converted into commercial property. At the front tall white columns flocked each side. Big bay windows sat on either side of the front doors. Each one was filled with gorgeous wedding dresses on display. Entering the store, it was even fancier. Marble floors, large chandeliers hung from the ceiling and dresses filled the floor. Before I could take in anymore, a young woman approached me.

"Good afternoon, welcome to Grand Lush Bridal Salon. My name is Alexis. Are you looking for a dress?"

"Good afternoon. No, I'm looking for Annie Price. Is she available?" I asked.

"I can see if she is available. May I have your name please?" she asked.

"Leah Jordan," I replied.

"While you wait, would you like some cucumber water?" Alexis asked.

Eww. "No, thank you, I'm fine," I replied.

"If you want to take a seat over on the couch, she'll be down in a few minutes," Alexis instructed.

I looked over to the couch she was referring to. This was not just any couch. It was one of the fanciest couches I've ever seen. With a high back and ornate details along the sides and at the top, I felt like I was sitting on something you would find in a castle. A few minutes later, Annie descended one of the two spiral staircases. She appeared to be in good spirits given the current circumstances.

"Ms. Jordan, it's nice to see you. How can I help you?" Annie asked.

"Good to see you again also. Do you have some time to talk?" I asked.

"Let me just talk to one of my managers and I'll be right back," Annie replied.

Annie strode over to one of the long front counters and spoke to one of her employees. Then she returned to me and motioned for me to follow her. We headed up the spiral staircase to the left, past rows and rows of dresses towards a small office.

Annie led me into Vanessa's office. "Please, have a seat," she instructed.

"Thank you," I said taking a seat.

The desk was filled with paperwork, various binders, and folders.

"Sorry about the mess. It's been a little hectic since..." Annie's voice began to crack.

"It's okay, I understand. How have you been doing?" I asked.

"Holding up. We've been busy with homecoming and Winter formals coming up on top of our normal bridal business," Annie replied.

"I wanted to stop by to let you know, I've decided to look into what happened to Vanessa," I explained.

She gave me a shocked look. "You are? Why?"

"Do you remember the death of the guy buy the CEO of Body by Mimi a few months ago?" I asked.

"Yeah, I think so. Why?" Annie asked.

"I helped in solving the case," I replied.

"The police said they have a suspect I thought?"

"I know, but I'm not bad at investigating and I feel a responsibility to do something since Vanessa was one of our vendors," I explained.

"That's so nice of you. What can I do to help?" Annie asked.

"How about you start by telling me how you know Vanessa? I know you've known each other for a long time and outside of the bridal salon," I said.

"Wow, you know that? She and I attended high school together. We were kindred spirits. Vanessa and I both came from households that didn't have a lot. We weren't the most popular girls and bonded over that," Annie explained.

"Can you think of anyone who would want to hurt Vanessa?" I asked.

"I've been thinking about that. I'm not sure, she and I lost track for a while when she moved to New York City. Maybe someone from that part of her life?" Annie suggested.

"That's a possibility. Did she have problems with anyone you know?" I asked.

"Now that I think about it, there has been an ongoing issue with the landlord for this building," Annie replied.

"Vanessa doesn't own the building then. What was the issue?" I asked.

"No, she decided to lease it to spend more on décor and remodeling the place. Vanessa didn't share many details with me, but since she's gone, I've reviewed the books and realized we're behind on rent payments. I even found an unpleasant letter from him. I gave the police the original, but I kept a copy. Let me find it," Annie said.

"What is the landlord's name?" I asked.

"Ed Garver," Annie responded. "Ah! Here it is." Annie handed me the letter.

I skimmed it quickly. "How can I get a hold of him?"

"Do you think he could have hurt Vanessa?" Annie asked.

"I don't know, but if they had an issue with each other, we need to get to the bottom of it," I explained.

"I see. Let me see if I can find his contact information," Annie said.

Annie grabbed a slim hard-bound book from one of the piles and began flipping through. "Vanessa kept all her phone numbers and addresses in this. Here it is. His phone number is 555-2348."

I wrote the number down along with his name. "Got it, thank you."

"No problem," Annie replied.

"So, my next question may be a little sensitive, but I need to ask. What do you know about Vanessa seeing someone on the side?"

Annie's face turned red. "I didn't think anyone knew about that."

Oh boy. "It's true then?"

She looked down and began to wring her hands. "Yes, she was. No one was supposed to know, not even me. I stopped by her house one day to drop off some documents she needed to sign, and he was there. Vanessa swore me to secrecy, and she said she'd fire me if I told anyone. I needed my job, so I kept my mouth shut."

I had to tread lightly. "Do you know his name or any details about him?" I asked.

"The only thing I know is that his first name is Emilio. Vanessa said the less I knew, the better," Annie replied.

"So, you didn't see him during the bridal show at any time?" I asked.

"I don't recall that, but it doesn't mean he wasn't at some point," Annie said.

"Did Vanessa's fiancé have any idea?"

"No, I don't think so. He never said anything to me."

The intercom on the phone buzzed. "Annie, it's Erin, I hate to bother you, but we have a delivery here and there's an issue. Can you please come down to the back?" Erin sked.

"Of course, Erin, I'll be right there," Annie responded as she hit the button. "I'm sorry, Ms. Jordan, I need to cut this short, I hope you understand."

"Of course, not a problem. I appreciate you talking to me. If you think of anything else, give me a call," I said standing up.

"I will. Thank you. Let me walk you back down."

Annie stood up, walked to the office door, and held it open, waiting for me to step out first. When we reached the front, she paused to speak with another one of her employees before heading towards the back. Although I learned more than before, I didn't get to ask everything I wanted to. Still, I had a couple of leads, which would keep me moving forward for now.

CHAPTER TEN

Checking my watch, I decided to stop and get an iced coffee before deciding what to do next. I also ordered a cherry Danish for a quick sugar rush. Pulling into the parking lot, I plucked the Danish from the bag and broke off a piece. Oh. My. Word. It was so good.

Feeling refreshed and re-energized, I decided to check in with Caleb and see if he wanted to join me. I pulled my phone out and dialed his number.

"Hey Jordan, I was just about to call you, what's up?" Caleb asked as he answered the phone.

"Just finished meeting with Annie Price. Thought I would see if you were available and wanted to join me on some investigating?" I asked.

"Sounds good. I've finished up my tasks for the day. Where did you want to meet?" Caleb asked.

"Why don't I send you the address for Mrs. DiCarlo's, and then we'll go from there?"

"Perfect, text the address and I'll meet you there."

"Great. See you then."

I hung up and texted Caleb before driving again. While I drove, I began thinking of what I needed to ask Mrs. DiCarlo. Hopefully, she had more information on Vanessa's mystery man. Turning on the street, I scanned the street trying to see if there were any cars at Vanessa's. None appeared in the driveway.

I found an open spot on the street, a few doors down from Mrs. DiCarlo's. Exiting my car, I shut the door and leaned against the driver's side while I waited for Caleb. Five minutes later, I noticed Caleb's silver rental sedan coming down the street. I waved at him as he parked. Caleb met me at my car, and we headed down the sidewalk to Mrs. DiCarlo's. There were no cars in the driveway. A neighbor next door was working in their flower beds.

"Does she know we're coming?" Caleb asked.

"No, I figured we would just stop by unannounced, then she won't be able to prepare her answers," I replied.

Caleb laughed. "Ah, the good ol' winging it method."

I smacked his arm and shrugged. "It's been successful this far; I figure why change now."

We stepped up to Mrs. DiCarlo's front door and knocked.

We waited a few minutes and there was no answer. I knocked again. Nada. Caleb looked through the front windows to see if he could see any movement.

"I don't see anyone in there, and I don't hear anything. Maybe she's not home," I murmured.

"Maybe. I'll leave one of my cards on her door," he suggested.

As we descended the stairs, the neighbor I had observed earlier approached us. "Are you looking for Mrs. DiCarlo?"

"Yes, ma'am, we are. Do you happen to know when she might be back?" Caleb asked.

"It's Thursday., She has a standing weekly appointment in Barton for a wash and set. Do you mind if I ask what this is regarding?" the neighbor asked.

"Of course, my name is Caleb Hamilton, and this is my associate, Leah Jordan. We are looking into the murder of Ms. Mitchell across the street and another neighbor told us she may have some pertinent information," Caleb explained.

"Oh, well I will let her know you stopped by. Is there a number or a way she can reach you?"

"We left a card on her door, but here's another one. We appreciate it. If you think of anything that might be important, please feel free to reach out to us also," Caleb explained while I handed her another card.

"Thank you. You two have a good day," she replied heading

back to her flower bed

I waited till the neighbor was out of earshot before talking. "Do you think she'll tell Mrs. DiCarlo we stopped by?"

"I think so. If not, we can try to stop by again if she doesn't respond in a day or so," Caleb replied.

"True. I have a couple more stops I wanted to make if you have the time?" I asked.

"Sure. Why don't we head to your office first and leave one of the cars, that way we can talk as we drive?" Caleb suggested.

"Great idea. Just follow me," I replied.

We made it to the Wedded Bliss and left Caleb's rental car behind. I ran in to let Sally know it would be in the parking lot so no one would think it was a suspicious vehicle and needed to be towed. Once we were back in my car, I decided to fill Caleb in on my conversation with Fannie.

"Last night, just as I was about to turn in, Fannie called me. She remembered that someone did see her Saturday night and that could be her alibi," I explained.

"Really? That's great! Who is it?" Caleb asked.

"Saturday night, Fannie ordered a pizza from Tony's, a local pizza joint. The delivery driver could attest to seeing her that night. I wanted to head there and see if we could talk to the driver. Fannie has her receipt also, which I will get from her later."

"Perfect, let's go."

We left the parking lot and traveled to Tony's. The building appeared like a large barn from the outside but had a typical Italian/pizzeria design. Once we arrived, the lunch rush was gone, and the parking lot was almost empty. Locally owned, Tony's had the best pizza in Ashford. The sauce was to die for.

Once we stepped inside, I turned to look at Caleb. "Let me take the lead, I went to high school with the owner's daughter."

Caleb nodded. "You're the boss Jordan."

We stepped up to the front counter.

"Welcome to Tony's, my name is Kara. What can I get for you?" the front counter girl asked.

"I'm here to see Mr. Biscardi. Is he free?" I asked.

"Let me check. I know he's around somewhere," she replied.

A few moments later, Mr. Biscardi came up front. A shoo-in for Luigi from Mario Brothers, he was tall and thin with dark hair and a big bushy mustache.

"Leah? Leah Jordan? I haven't seen you in forever," Mr. Biscardi said.

I smiled and shook his hand. "It's good to see you. This is my friend Caleb. We're here because I need your help with something."

"Why don't you tell me what you need, and I'll see what you can do," Mr. Biscardi replied.

"I'm not sure if you have heard about the murder that happened Saturday night?" I asked.

"I can't say that I have," Mr. Biscardi replied.

"I am looking into what happened and I need to see if you received a pizza order from Fannie Harrison on Saturday night," I explained.

"Flower shop Fannie? Why her?" Mr. Biscardi asked.

"We need to prove her alibi, and this would help us to clear her name," I replied.

"Anything for Fannie. She took such good care of us when my daughter got married last year. My daughter was over the moon with her work," Mr. Biscardi said.

"Fannie is one of a kind. The pizza was ordered between eight forty-five and nine p.m.," I said.

"It will take me a little time to review the order history. While you wait, would you guys like anything? How about a couple of slices of pizza and soft drinks?" Mr. Biscardi offered.

"Thanks, Mr. Biscardi. A couple of slices and drinks would be nice," I replied.

"Of course, have a seat and I'll have someone bring it out to you. Meanwhile, I'll go research Saturday's orders," Mr. Biscardi instructed.

Caleb and I took a seat at one of the two-person tables.

"How did you do that?" Caleb asked.

"What do you mean?" I asked.

"You just asked, and he agreed to help. That's not normal,"

he replied.

I shrugged. "Guess there is something to be said for small towns."

"Yeah, I guess so."

One of the servers brought over our pizza slices and drinks. "Enjoy," she said.

It grew quiet and Caleb just sat there looking at the massive slice on his plate.

"It's not going to bite you, try it," I said.

"I can't decide if I should cut it up first," Caleb replied.

I laughed. "Let me show you the best way to eat at Tony's." I picked the slice up, folded it in half and took a big bite.

Caleb followed suit. "Wow, this pizza is so good!"

"I told you," I said between bites.

"You did, you were right," Caleb said.

I laughed. "Can I have that in writing Hamilton?"

"Ha. Ha. You're so funny," he replied.

After we finished our food, Mr. Biscardi returned to our table.

"I found the order and printed a couple of copies," Mr. Biscardi said.

"Great, thank you. Do you know the driver that took the run?" I asked.

Mr. Biscardi scanned one of the papers he held. "Let's see, it was Kyle, Kyle Wilson."

"Is Kyle working today?" Caleb asked.

"It's his day off. He attends Barton Community College a few days a week. I could give him your contact information and ask him to call you," Mr. Biscardi responded.

"That would be great. Let me get you one of my cards," I said reaching into my bag.

Mr. Biscardi took my card. "Great, I'll contact Kyle and have him contact you."

"Thank you for all your help and for our pizza and drinks. It's always so delicious!" I commented, reaching out to shake Mr. Biscardi's hand.

"Yes, thank you, sir." Caleb also shook his hand.

"You're welcome. Come back anytime," Mr. Biscardi said.

Caleb and I left the restaurant and headed back to my car.

"Now what?" Caleb asked.

"While we wait to hear from Kyle, I can fill you in about my conversation with Annie earlier," I answered.

He nodded. "Great, I'm interested in what she could tell you."

"It did get cut short, but I learned some things. As I discovered earlier, Annie and Vanessa had known each other from high school. She knew of Vanessa's guy on the side but didn't have much to tell me. However, she provided me with a first name, Emilio."

"It's not a common name so that's good. We should be able

to locate him more easily."

"I hope so. Then she told me about someone who was having an issue with Vanessa. The landlord of the Grand Lush Bridal Salon."

"What's the issue?"

"Vanessa was behind on her rent payments and the landlord wasn't happy with her," I explained.

"Can you blame him?" Caleb asked.

"Would that make someone want to kill? Seems like it was the case, murders would be on the rise."

"You never know. Remember every lead -- big or small -- is worth looking into."

"I brought his address with me. Do you have time for another stop?"

Caleb looked down at his watch and furrowed his brows. He probably had something more important to do. I looked away waiting for him to answer.

Finally, he spoke. "For you? Always."

"Are you sure? If you have something more important to do, I can..."

Caleb cut me off. "Stop, don't be silly. If I didn't want to help, I wouldn't be here."

"Great." I handed him my notebook. "I wrote the address down, can you please input that into your directions app while I start driving?"

"Sure."

Once Caleb pulled up the directions, we found out the landlord Mr. Garver's house was only a few minutes from the pizza shop. They led us to an older duplex on a quiet street. There were duplexes mixed in with homes all built back in the early 1920's. Most appeared to have been renovated while others were dilapidated, and a few were boarded up.

"Which one is his?" I asked.

Caleb pointed. "His is on the left."

I found a spot on the street to park. Caleb and I walked up the sidewalk to the front steps. Before we reached the top step, the front door opened.

"Can I help you?" a gentleman with medium-length gray and white hair, five o'clock shadow, wire-rimmed glasses and looking a little disheveled asked.

"Hello sir, we were looking for Ed Garver. Is he home by chance?" I asked.

"You found him, what can I do for you?" he asked with a smile.

"We were hoping you had a few minutes to talk?" I asked.

"I was just getting ready to head out, but I guess I could spare a few minutes," Mr. Garver replied.

"Thank you, sir, we appreciate it," I said.

"We wanted to ask you some questions about Vanessa Mitchell," Caleb said.

"What about her?" Mr. Garver groused.

His misdemeanor changed quickly, and you could tell this was a sore subject.

"We understand she rents the building her bridal salon is currently located in. Is that correct?" I asked.

"Yes, I am her landlord. Did they also tell you, that she is three months behind in rent?" Mr. Garver asked.

"Yes, they did mention that. What can you tell us about Vanessa Mitchell?" Caleb asked.

"She's a real piece of work, that girl. I didn't even want to lease to her at first, but she was relentless until I agreed," Ed replied.

"Why didn't you want to lease to her, if you don't mind me asking?" I asked.

"She was going to carry all these fancy dresses; I just didn't see how people in Ashford would afford them. Against my better judgment, I gave in. Things were fine at first. Then this past year, things became rocky. It started with a few late payments, then a missed payment. Vanessa promised she had it and would get it to me. When I called her about it, she began avoiding my calls --" Mr. Garver explained.

"Were you ever able to talk to her about it?" Caleb asked.

"Yes, eventually, I stopped by the store one day and caught her off guard. All she had were a bunch of excuses and empty promises," Mr. Garver said.

"So, you were pretty angry with her?" I asked.

Mr. Garver threw his hands up in exasperation. "Who wouldn't be? I'm a retired veteran. I don't get paid much. I can't even pay my bills to live."

"Did you explain that to her?" Caleb asked.

Mr. Garver looked at Caleb as if he had just heard that the sky was purple. "Of course! Any decent person would apologize, try and make things right, but not her."

"What happened next?" I asked.

Mr. Garver hung his head slightly and let out a loud sigh. "My temper got the best of me and I raised my voice. That's when some guy built like a tank stepped in, so I left and told her that I was filing eviction paperwork with the court."

"It never got physical at any point though?" Caleb asked.

"No. I may have a short temper, but I know that it's best to walk away and calm down. You see, I suffer from PTSD, and I've been taking anger management classes and therapy. Jeopardizing my freedom is not worth it. Hence why I decided to take the legal route and file eviction paperwork with the court when my other attempts to rectify the situation were not working," Mr. Garver answered.

"Do you know the gentleman that stepped in?" I asked.

"Vanessa said his name was Milo, Leo, something like that. She said he was her landscaper. I'm not sure why he was at the bridal salon. I handle the landscaping for my properties," Mr.

Garver replied.

"Where were you last Saturday evening?' Caleb asked.

"I was at one of my meetings at the Trinity Baptist Church in Barton. Why is that important?" Mr. Garver asked.

"Vanessa Mitchell was murdered Saturday evening," I replied.

"And you think I had something to do with that?" Mr. Garver grumbled.

"Not necessarily, but we have to talk to everyone who knew Ms. Mitchell," Caleb advised.

"Like I said, I value my freedom and my life too much to do something so stupid. You're not a landlord for over twenty years without dealing with crappy tenants. Now if I've answered all your questions, I'd like to leave before I'm late," Mr. Garver said.

"Of course. Thank you for your time, Mr. Garver," I said.

Mr. Garver walked past us down the stairs, got in his car, and drove down the street. Caleb and I followed suit and headed back to my car.

"That was intense," I said as I started the car.

"I feel his bark is worse than his bite," Caleb commented.

"Maybe. He did give us another clue to Vanessa's side piece, he's a landscaper," I said.

"Which should help further in narrowing it down. Also, it would be good to verify Mr. Garver's alibi."

"Of course. Let's see, we need to talk to Mrs. DiCarlo, the delivery driver Kyle, get the receipt from Fannie, and keep searching for the mystery lover. Did you hear back on any of the financial reports yet?" I asked.

"I've heard back on Annie Price. Nothing questionable or worrisome. Some credit card debt and a school loan she is paying back," Caleb replied.

"What about Vanessa?"

"Funny you should ask. It doesn't make sense, especially after what you learned earlier. Her finances are in order."

"Things get weirder and weirder as we go. What about Hoyt Walker?" I asked.

"He is the one we are still waiting on," Caleb answered.

"I don't know about you, but I'm feeling pretty beat for today. I just want to grab some dinner and relax."

"I don't blame you. I have some work I should do back at my hotel."

"I'll take you to your car," I said.

"Sounds good. We'll check in with each other tomorrow?" Caleb asked.

"Yeah, that works for me."

I dropped Caleb off at his car. Everyone else had left the Wedded Bliss for the day, so I headed home. My stomach started growling. After getting home, I headed straight for the kitchen to find food.

The pickings were slim. The slice of pizza earlier wasn't holding any longer. As I rooted through the fridge, I snatched a chunk of cheese, some summer sausage and grabbed a box of wheat crackers from the pantry. I made up a little snack plate and took it to the front room.

After getting settled, I began thinking about everything that I had done so far. There were several people that had a motive and the only one we've been able to clear was Fannie. Which was great, but it still meant a murderer was loose in Ashford.

Nibbling on a cracker with cheese, I also began thinking about the Wedded Bliss. It felt like I hadn't seen Meg and Chelsea in forever. Before they started despising me, it was best we met and caught up. I texted Meg, Chelsea, and Sally to let them know I was bringing breakfast in for everyone for tomorrow's meeting. I finished eating and my mind finally relaxed. After dropping my plate off in the kitchen, I crawled into bed and passed out.

CHAPTER ELEVEN

Staying true to my word, I stopped at Ashford's Diner the next morning. The first thing that caught my eye was the dessert case near the front counter. I picked up sausage patties, scrambled eggs, pancakes, and fruit salad. My car smelled divine. It was hard not to pull over and scarf some of it down.

Arriving at the Wedded Bliss, I parked as close to the front door as possible and grabbed the food bags from the back seat. Juggling the bags and my purse, I unlocked the front door and headed inside. Turning on the lights, I dropped off the food in the conference room. Then I went down to the kitchen to gather plates, small bowls, napkins silverware, and glasses.

Checking the fridge, I found a carton of orange juice and grabbed that, too. Taking everything back to the conference room, I set the table. Then, I pulled the food from the bags and arranged it. Once it was finished, I waited for the others to arrive.

Meg arrived first, with Sally following soon after.

"Leah? Are you here?" Meg called out.

"In the conference room, just follow the smell," I yelled.

A few minutes later, they entered the room.

"Wow, this looks amazing Leah!" Meg exclaimed.

"You are too much Leah," Sally murmured.

"Oh hush. I've been so busy investigating and you guys have been holding it down here, it's the least I could do," I replied.

"We know you're trying to help Fannie and that's important," Meg responded.

"Thank you. Any idea where Chelsea is?" I asked.

Sally clucked. "You know her, perpetually late."

Just then she sauntered in. "Hey now, I heard that."

"Come in and get some food before it gets cold," I instructed.

Chelsea saluted. "Yes ma'am!"

We all filled our plates and settled down at the table. A few minutes went by before any of us spoke, we were all so busy stuffing our faces.

"I think this has to be one of the best ideas you've had," Chelsea said in between bites.

"I have to agree. This is delicious!" Sally exclaimed.

"Thank you. Since I've been so preoccupied with investigating, why don't you fill me in on what's going on with you guys?" I asked.

"I'm just trying to survive. This new mom stuff is no joke. I'm not sure I'm cut out for it," Meg responded and let out a deep sigh.

"Oh, Meg! You are doing a great job and will be an awesome mother. Don't be so hard on yourself! You know if you need anything, you only need to ask. Even if it's just someone to come sit with Delaney just so you can get a nap, we would be glad to do it," I said.

"Hey now, don't toss me into that group. You know I can barely take care of myself, let alone a baby," Chelsea interjected.

"Oh jeez. You can run errands for her then," I replied.

"That I can do," Chelsea conceded.

"You know I love babies, call me anytime," Sally piped up.

I smiled at Meg. "See? We have your back."

Meg began to tear up. "Thanks, guys. I didn't realize how tired I would be and how hard work it is, but I love that little girl so much."

"I have a little news," Sally piped up.

"Oh yeah? Tell us," I said.

"I met someone. His name is Paul, and we met at a cooking class the senior center had a couple of weeks ago," Sally replied.

We all awed.

"That is so wonderful!" Meg exclaimed.

"Way to go Sally!" Chelsea said waggling her eyebrows.

Sally waved her hands. "Now, now girls. We are taking this slowly. I haven't dated anyone since my husband passed and this is all new to me."

"Tell us more about him," I prodded.

"He's retired from the sawmill, divorced, has two adult children and owns a place on the outskirts of town towards Barton. He has some land, a little pond and raises chickens and sells eggs at the Farmer's market," Sally replied.

"He sounds great. We can't wait to meet him," Meg said.

"I am so happy for you," I said.

"Me too," Chelsea added.

Sally smiled and appeared to glow. "Thanks girls. I appreciate it."

"What's new in your world Chelsea?" I asked.

"Funny you should ask. I have a situation, things are a little rough right now," Chelsea replied.

"A little rough, what do you mean?" I asked.

She let out a big sigh. "I don't even know if I can say it out loud."

"Oh, it can't be that bad. You can tell us anything," Meg said.

"Alex...Alex wants me to..." Chelsea's voice trailed off and the rest of the words were all mumbled.

"Say that again, and speak clearer this time," I instructed.

"Alex wants me to meet...meet his family!" Chelsea exclaimed, putting her head in her hands.

"That's it? What's wrong with that?" Meg asked.

"Yeah, you guys have been together for a few months now, that's par for the course my friend," I said.

She blew a raspberry. "Not for me, Chelsea Baker. I usually don't date anyone a few weeks let alone a few months."

"Exactly. There is something different about Alex whether you want to admit it to yourself or not," Meg said.

"What do I do?" Chelsea moaned.

"Tell Alex you would love to meet his parents," I responded.

Chelsea let out a long sigh. "Do you know how long it's been since I've met anyone's parents? What do I wear? What do I say?"

"Just be yourself. They will love you as much as we do," Meg said.

"Find something to take as a thank you. A nice bottle of wine, a pie, or pastries from Bonnie's or flowers from Fannie's. His mom will love the gesture, and you'll earn some brownie points," I suggested.

"Those are good ideas and some great advice. Speaking of Fannie, what is going on with the case?" Chelsea asked.

"There seem to be several people with motives, but I haven't been able to narrow it down to just one. The more interviews and investigating, the closer we'll get," I replied.

"What about Fannie? Did you find out if she has an alibi?" Sally asked.

"She does. Which reminds me, I need to call her later and ask her to stop by," I said.

"Who else could have done that to Ms. Mitchell?" Meg asked.

"Get this, she had a fiancé and a guy on the side," I replied.

Everyone gasped.

"You're kidding me!" Meg exclaimed.

"Oh my," Sally murmured.

"Not sure how she was able to juggle it all, but we have gotten only a little information about him. He's a little bit of a mystery," I explained.

"Who else are you looking at?" Chelsea asked.

"There is Vanessa's landlord. Apparently, they have been feuding because she is several months behind in rent. The fiancé, the woman who was here protesting, and her assistant," I said ticking off each one on my fingers.

"Her assistant? She seemed like such a lovely girl. A little timid, but very sweet," Sally commented.

"We can't count anyone out yet, except Fannie of course. Enough about me, this breakfast was to spend time with you and catch up on what's happening here," I replied.

"Remember that couple who wanted the Beauty and the Beast themed wedding?" Sally asked.

"Oh yes, Aubrey and Trent," I replied.

"They called back to book their wedding with us!" Sally

exclaimed.

I threw my fist in the air. "That's awesome! They are such a sweet couple. I look forward to working with them."

"I've been working on new marketing ideas, including posting ads on our Facebook page and following up with the bridal show vendors to develop potential cross-promotion opportunities," Chelsea explained.

"How about you. Meg?" I asked.

"I'm glad you asked. I've been working on creating a newsletter. I thought it would allow us to keep in contact with potential and former clients and provide wedding-related information and tips. For example, we could have a theme and include small articles in each one. You could even write a little note or letter at the beginning," Meg replied.

"That's a great idea. Both are. Whatever you need me to do, just let me know," I replied.

"I'm glad you like them. This breakfast was exactly what we needed. Thank you," Meg said.

"Yes, it's so good. I'll have to hit the gym later," Chelsea said.

I rolled my eyes. "Oh please! You are in such good shape. One big breakfast will not hurt."

Chelsea stuck her tongue out at me.

Sally checked her watch. "It's almost time to open. If you guys want to get ready for the day, I'll clean up."

"Sounds great, thank you so much. I need to go catch up on

my emails and messages," I replied.

"Of course. You ladies have a great day," Sally said.

Chelsea, Meg, and I headed to our perspective offices, while Sally remained in the conference room. Once at my desk, I turned my computer on and waited for it to boot up. Pulling up my email, I was shocked. I normally don't have that many emails. I skimmed the inbox, deleting spam and ads.

The remainder appeared to be inquiries from potential clients. I picked up my notepad to make a list of people to reply to and set it aside. I grabbed the stack of messages Sally left on my desk and began flipping through them. To my surprise, there was a message to return from Mrs. DiCarlo, and another from Kyle, the delivery driver from Tony's.

Deciding to answer the emails first, I responded to each one to gather more information and offered to set up in-person appointments if they were interested. It took a couple of hours and once everyone had been responded to, it was time to grab a fresh cup of coffee. My next priority was to reach out to Fannie and get the receipt.

Back in my office, I dialed her number.

"Hello?" Fannie answered.

"Hey Fannie, it's Leah. I'm so sorry I didn't get hold of you yesterday. I was wondering if I could get that receipt."

"No problem, Leah. I'm out picking up lunch right now. I could come by your office in about ten to fifteen minutes if that works for you?" Fannie asked.

"I'll see you then," I replied.

The call disconnected and I followed up on a couple more messages while I waited for her to arrive. My office phone intercom beeped.

"Leah, can you come up front, please? Fannie is here," Sally called.

"I'll be up in just a minute. Thank you," I responded.

As I headed to the front, I could hear them deep in conversation.

"I can't believe you have to go through this," Sally said.

"It hasn't been easy. I'm just so glad you asked Leah to help me. Who knows what would have happened," Fannie said.

I cleared my throat as I approached them. "Hello, ladies. I appreciate you coming Fannie."

"Of course. Like I said, whatever you need from me to help, I'm willing to do," she replied.

"Can I see the receipt please?" I asked.

Fannie reached into her pants pocket and pulled out a folded credit card slip. "Here you go."

Taking a few seconds to look it over, it matched the copy of the order Tony provided us. Perfect.

"Let me take a copy of this and I'll bring it right back," I instructed.

"Sure thing," Fannie replied.

Heading down the hallway to our copy machine, I made a couple copies and went back up front. "Here you go," I said, handing it back to Fannie.

"Thank you, I appreciate what you're doing to help me. If you need anything else, please let me know." Fannie checked her watch. "I better get back to the shop. I have a big floral order I need to finish."

"I will. Take care and we'll talk soon," I replied.

Back settled in my office, I contacted Kyle, the delivery driver, to get the last part we needed to solidify Fannie's alibi. After dialing his number, a loud heavy metal song came over. In shock, I almost hung up.

"You've reached Kyle," his voice came across the line.

"Hi, sorry. This is Leah Jordan. I was returning your call," I explained.

"Oh hey. Yeah, Mr. Biscardi told me you had some questions for me about a delivery I made or something," Kyle replied.

"Yes, that's correct. It would have been this past Saturday night. The customer was Fannie Harrison. Do you remember delivering to her?" I asked.

"I do," Kyle replied.

"How can you be so sure? I imagine you make a lot of deliveries, especially on a busy Saturday night," I asked.

"Oh, Mrs. Harrison is one of my favorite clients. She always tips well, and I remember delivering to her the other night because I asked her advice on what flowers she recommended I get my girlfriend for our first anniversary," Kyle explained.

"Great. That is what I needed to know. Thank you so much for your time," I said.

"You're welcome. Have a good day," Kyle replied.

Hanging up the phone, a huge sense of relief came over me. Fannie could officially be marked off the suspect list. One down, more to go. Pulling up the browser on my computer, I decided to search for local landscape companies. A town the size of Ashford, there couldn't be that many.

chapter twelve

To my surprise, there were a lot more results than I expected. I wrote down the company names and phone numbers. I tried the first few companies, and none had any employees named Emilio. Before I could continue down the list, one of the potential brides returned my call. We set up an appointment and tour.

I checked the time, and it was almost two o'clock. It was imperative to keep calling landscapers. A couple of calls later, I was still striking out. The sixth company on the list was called Landscape D-sign. The phone rang and all I could hear were people talking in the background. There was some static, and finally, a person spoke.

"You've reached Landscape D-sign. This is Tasha, how may I help you?" she asked.

"Hi, my name is Leah, and I was interested in having some

landscaping work done," I explained.

"Bye! See you later," Tasha said.

What? Was she talking to me? "Excuse me?"

"Oh, sorry, honey. What did you say again?"

"I was calling to find out about getting some landscaping done. My girlfriend told me about a guy named Emilio and how great his work is. Does he have any availability?" I asked.

"Emilio? I think you have the wrong landscape company, ma'am. We don't have anyone here by that name," Tasha replied.

"I'm sorry. Thank you for your time," I responded and hung up.

This was like playing a game of hide and seek and I wasn't winning. The next company on the list had a disconnected number. That left Ashford Lawn Care, LLC. Crossing my fingers, I dialed their number.

"Thank you for calling Ashford Lawn Care, LLC. This is Sheri. How may we help you with your lawn care needs?" the receptionist asked.

"Hi Sheri, my name is Leah, and I was interested in some possible landscaping at my home. One of my girlfriends recommended your company to me. She mentioned Emilio was excellent. Would he be available?" I asked.

She laughed, then cleared her throat. "Sorry, I didn't mean to laugh but Emilio is one of our most popular landscapers."

Bingo! "That's a good thing, right?" I asked.

"Not sure if your friend mentioned it, but he's very easy on the eyes. You may not want to use him if you have a jealous boyfriend or husband," Sheri advised.

"Not a problem, I'm single." I chuckled.

"Great. He usually books up fast. How soon were you interested in setting up a consultation?" she asked.

"As soon as possible would be great, thank you," I replied.

"Give me a few minutes to check our calendar and see what's available," Sheri said. The line grew quiet, and I could hear the clackety-clack of her computer keys. "Okay, ma'am, it looks like we have an open consultation slot a couple of days from now, Thursday at ten in the morning. Would that work for you?"

"That would be perfect," I said.

"Great. If you give me your full name, address, and phone number, I'll put you on the appointment calendar," Sheri instructed.

I provided her with the information. Sheri advised that I would be receiving a reminder text the day before. Finally, the search was over. Now, I had to figure out what Emilio had to say for himself and whether he had anything to do with Vanessa's death. I decided to call Mrs. DiCarlo back before it got too much later.

She picked up on the second ring. "Hello?"

"Good afternoon, is this Mrs. DiCarlo?" I asked.

"Yes," she replied.

"Mrs. DiCarlo, my name is Leah Jordan. I was returning your message," I said.

"Oh yes, you're the one who left a card on my door and with my neighbor."

"Yes ma'am. I wanted to stop by and talk to you about your neighbor, Ms. Mitchell," I explained.

"That two-bit floozy? What about her?" Mrs. DiCarlo questioned.

Wow. She didn't mince words. "I can explain better in person. If you're home now, I could stop by," I responded.

Mrs. DiCarlo didn't speak for a few seconds. "Fine, but you have to be done before my programs come on."

"Of course. I promise I won't take up too much of your time. Thank you. I'll see you soon," I replied.

"Goodbye," Mrs. DiCarlo replied before hanging up.

I turned off my computer, gathered my notebook, and straightened up my desk. Reaching out to Caleb, I wanted to see if he wanted to join.

"Hey Jordan," Caleb answered.

"I just got off the phone with Mrs. DiCarlo. She's home and willing to meet. Want to meet me there? If you're not busy that is," I asked.

"Sure. I'll meet you there," Caleb replied.

"See you then," I said.

When the door opened, I didn't know what to expect. Mrs. DiCarlo was approximately five feet three inches tall, wearing a big orange turban on her head, black-rimmed glasses, large brown hoop earrings, a long flowery-patterned caftan, and orange palazzo pants with wedge sandals. Her arms were filled with a mix of skinny and chunky wood and metal bracelets. Every time she moved, the bracelets jangled.

"Are you Leah?" she asked.

"Yes, and this is my associate, Caleb Hamilton." I gestured towards him. "May we come in?" I asked.

Mrs. DiCarlo gave us both the once over as to size us up and determine if we were dangerous or not. "Come on in. Please take your shoes off before entering my Zen area," she instructed.

Caleb and I looked at each other and then did as she requested. We followed her into a large living room that was filled with all kinds of colorful tapestries on the wall. There were also several types of silk fabrics draped around the room. If there had been a table with a crystal ball in the middle of the room,

I would have thought we were visiting a fortune teller. Mrs. DiCarlo gestured for us to sit on big, round floor pillows.

"Now that we're settled, what can I do for you?" Mrs. DiCarlo asked.

"How long have you known Ms. Mitchell?" I asked.

"Too long. She moved in about four or five years ago. I could tell her aura was not positive. Now there will be harmony again on this street. While we were not close, the news of her sudden passing is sad. No one should leave this earth before their time," she replied.

She was out there. I had to stifle a laugh. "What made you not like Ms. Mitchell?"

"Where do I begin? The loud parties, never bringing up her trash cans, cars always blocking the street, people parking in front of my house, and others. She was very inconsiderate. I complained to the home association several times," Mrs. DiCarlo explained.

"Did anything improve?" Caleb asked.

"Oh, she would come over, make nicey nice and things would be good for a while, then it was the same old thing."

"When was the last time you saw Ms. Mitchell?" I asked.

"I believe it was last week sometime. She had that 'friend' of hers over in the landscaping truck and he blocked my mailbox. I didn't get my mail that day and I was expecting an important letter. Not the first time that's happened," Mrs. DiCarlo replied.

"This 'friend' of hers, what can you tell us about him?" Caleb asked.

"He's one of those muscle guys. A real thinks he's god's gift to women type but dumb as a box of rocks. He tried to come over here once and schmooze me into signing up for his services, but I wasn't having it." She briefly stopped talking and looked at both of us. "You realize when I say 'friend', I mean that they were making whoopie, right?"

"Yes, we have heard their relationship was more than friendly," Caleb commented.

"Did you witness anything suspicious last Saturday night? Was the landscaping truck there that evening?" I asked.

"No. The truck wasn't there that night, but I saw a car on the street. I didn't recognize it," Mrs. DiCarlo replied.

"Could you describe it?" Caleb asked.

"It was dark, and the car was a blue or black SUV. The windows were tinted, so I couldn't tell if anyone was inside," she replied.

"About what time would you say you witnessed the car out there?" I asked.

"Hmm, probably around ten thirty. I was finishing my nightly meditation and then I heard arguing. I got up to see what was going on but by the time I got to the front windows, I didn't see anyone, it was quiet. The next morning, the SUV was gone. Then later that day is when I saw the cops show up," she responded.

"Did you speak with the cops?" Caleb asked.

"Yes, I thought they were here following up on one of my complaints, so I walked over to talk to them. That's when one of the officers informed me it was a crime scene and asked me to return to my residence," Mrs. DiCarlo explained.

"Is there anyone you can think of who would want to harm Ms. Mitchell?" I asked.

"My feelings are strong that the muscle head was involved. Her fiancé Hoyt is just the sweetest man, and I don't think he had anything to do with it. He always brought my trash and recycling cans up if I wasn't home and shoveled my driveway and sidewalk when it snowed. It's hard to find a decent man like that these days. I never understood what he saw in that woman," Mrs. DiCarlo responded.

"Is there anything else you can think of regarding Ms. Mitchell?" Caleb asked.

"No, not at the moment," she answered.

"We appreciate your time Mrs. DiCarlo. You have provided us with some great information. We'll contact you if we have any further questions," I said.

"Okay. Let me walk you two out then," she replied.

We put our shoes back on and walked out to my car. Mrs. Di Carlo watched us until we returned to our cars and drove off.

I had Caleb follow me so we could park and debrief.

"I have to say that was one of the strangest interviews I've had," Caleb commented.

"She didn't like Vanessa much, did she?" I asked.

Caleb shook his head. "No, no, she didn't. Mrs. DiCarlo may be eccentric, but we learned some good information."

"Now we need to figure out whose car that was she witnessed outside Saturday night," I said.

"If you want, I can do some research at the BMV and request a list of people in the area that owns vehicles similar to the one she witnessed," Caleb offered.

"Great idea," I replied.

"I better get started now. It could take a while and there are a couple of tasks I need to get done for my other clients," Caleb said.

"Not a problem. It has been another long day. We'll talk later," I said.

"Perfect," Caleb said.

CHAPTER THIRTEEN

Although we'd gone our separate ways, I was still too keyed up. I didn't want to go home, nor did I know what to do. Checking my watch, it was about the same time we were at Mr. Garver's the day prior, and he was heading to his meeting. Looking up the directions for the Trinity Baptist Church, I decided to take a chance and check it out.

The traffic was heavy, but I was able to make it to the church in twenty to twenty-five minutes. The parking lot was about half full. I found a spot near the middle of the lot and parked. Hopefully, there would be a sign or directory inside. I strode toward the front door.

To my left, there was a small café, and several hallways branched off in different directions. I must have looked confused and lost because, before I knew it, a middle-aged woman tapped me on the shoulder.

"Good evening miss, my name is Noreen. Can I help you?"

"Hello, I'm sorry, I was just trying to find a meeting. I thought I had the room number saved in my phone, but I can't find it," I explained hoping my clueless answer seemed plausible.

"No worries, dear! Were you looking for Alcoholics Anonymous? Narcotics Anonymous? Weight Watchers? New Mom's support group? Or our PTSD support group?" Noreen asked.

Wow, they were very welcoming to the community. "I was looking for the PTSD support group," I replied.

"That's in room seventeen. Just follow the hallway over on your right to the end of the hall and the room will be on your right," she instructed.

I smiled. "Great, thank you."

I traveled down the hall and found the room just as she had instructed. The door was slightly open. Stepping in, I tried to be as quiet as possible. A little music stand sat to my left with a binder containing sign-in sheets. There was a wall divider blocking the rest of the room.

I looked around to make sure no one was coming and then walked over to the music stand. Flipping back through the book, I located yesterday's sheets and began skimming them for Mr. Garver's signature. There were almost two and a half pages. Just as I was halfway down the second page, there it was.

He was telling the truth. Flipping the pages back to today's, I left it as I found it and crept backward out of the room. I looked to my left and witnessed Noreen standing in the front hall. She was talking to someone and facing away from me.

Looking both ways, I noticed an exit sign further down the hall to my right. I headed towards the end and opened the door. Oof! As I flung the door open, it hit something solid. When I looked up, Mr. Garver was standing there.

"Oh my gosh! I am so sorry!" I exclaimed.

"It's you! Are you following me?" Mr. Garver asked angrily.

"No-no, not at all," I stuttered.

"Then why are you here?"

Think fast Leah, think fast. "I work with several local brides and am looking for new churches to include on my local vendor's list."

His eyebrows were raised. "That's convenient. I thought you were an investigator?"

"I do that as well. Working on behalf of a friend," I replied.

Mr. Garver grew quiet as if to decide whether to believe me. Before he could speak again, another person entered the door behind him. I took the opportunity to slip past them and hurry to my car. I didn't look back until my car started.

My heart was still racing when I pulled into my driveway. Once I went inside, the cats were all over me. They were meowing loudly, rubbing against my legs, and making figure eights.

"Hello, ladies. Are you trying to tell me you're hungry?" I asked.

"Meow," Patches replied. That was a yes.

I dropped my bags and headed to the kitchen. Perusing the pantry, I grabbed a couple of cans of cat food from the shelf. I took half of the chicken and placed half on each plate. Repeating with the fish, I took a fork and mixed them up. Before I could get Patches bowl down, on the floor, she was trying to knock the dish out of my hand with her paw.

I laughed. "Excuse me, am I not going fast enough for you?"

She just looked at me and gave me the stink eye. Once they were scarfing down their food, I began looking for something for myself. Settling on a frozen dinner, I plopped it into the microwave and started the timer. After it was ready, I grabbed it out and headed into the living room to try and unwind.

My night ended up being very restless. At some point, I must have stumbled into my bedroom. When I opened my eyes, Oreo was on my chest and kneading me. Looking over at my alarm clock, it read six o'clock. Groaning, I tossed the covers over my head and rolled over. The peace didn't last long as the cats sensed a sign of life. Patches began meowing and licking my ear.

"Okay, okay! I'm getting up. Sheesh," I groused.

Flinging the covers off, I stumbled into the kitchen to start the coffeemaker. Heading to the bathroom, I took a steamy hot shower, letting the water beat down on my body. After drying off and getting dressed, I felt more alive. Swinging back through the kitchen, I poured a travel mug full of coffee and left for the office.

"Leah, good morning!" Sally exclaimed as I entered the door.

"Morning to you too! You're in a good mood. Did someone see her man last night?" I waggled my eyebrows.

Sally's face grew red. "Is it that obvious?"

"Yes, but it's sweet. I'm happy you're so happy," I replied.

"Thank you. It's nice having someone to do stuff with again. I've missed it," she grinned.

"Good. You deserve to be happy. I'm going to do some work. I'll check in later," I said.

"See you later," Sally replied.

As I trekked down the hall, Meg popped her head out of her office. "Hey, could you come in for a few minutes?"

"Sure, what's up?" I asked.

"I have a first draft or mock-up if you will of the newsletter. I wanted to get your thoughts," Meg answered.

"That's great. I'd love to see what you have so far," I said following her into her office.

She pulled up a second chair behind her desk and asked me to sit beside her. '

Meg opened the file. "Like I said, this is just a rough draft. The first page will have our logo at the bottom. At the top will be the name of our newsletter, the month, year, and volume it is. The table of contents could be on the left or right side and your letter will be in the center."

"I think it looks great. Did you have any name ideas?" I asked.

"Not yet. Any suggestions?" Meg asked.

"Let me think about it. I'll bring my ideas to the next morning's meeting. Sound good?" I asked.

"Sure. Maybe we can all submit a couple of name ideas, and then we can vote on the best one?" Meg suggested.

"What a perfect idea. I better get to my office. Keep working on the newsletter, it will be awesome," I said.

"Thank you! I am working on a list of topic proposals and will bring them to the meeting," Meg replied.

"Perfect!" I exclaimed.

Once I got settled at my desk, I pulled up my computer. I opened my email, and there were several replies from my follow-ups the day before. A couple of people just wanted further information, while a few others wanted to set up tours and consultations. I took time replying to each one and just as

I sent my last reply, my cell phone rang. It was Caleb.

"Hey, how are you?" I asked.

"Good. How are you?" Caleb replied.

"Not bad. What's up?" I replied.

"You know how we discussed getting a better idea or more knowledge about poisons?" Caleb asked.

"Yes, I do," I replied.

"I talked to a friend and she's willing to meet with us and give us some information on poisons," he explained.

"Really? That's great," I replied.

"Do you have time to meet later today? She is free at one o'clock," Caleb asked.

"It should be good. If something comes up, I can let you know."

"Oh no, it's a cake emergency! All forks on deck!" he laughed.

"Ha, ha. So funny Hamilton. You couldn't handle being a wedding planner. How's the car search going?" I asked.

He gasped. "What's that supposed to mean? I think I'd be great, thank you very much!"

"Mm-hmm, sure. I would love to see that," I teased. "You were going to tell me about the cars?"

"I found several results for that make and model. It's the narrowing down of the list that's going slowly. Who knew it was such a popular one? I've made some progress, but it'll take some time," Caleb replied.

"If I can help, let me know. We could make a game out of it," I said.

"I may take you upon that. I need to go, but I'll confirm our meeting and send you the details," Caleb said.

"Sounds good. I'll see you later," I replied before hanging up.

Caleb texted the confirmation of our meeting and the address, but I didn't pay too much attention until I was in my car ready to drive. The address seemed familiar, but it took me a few minutes to realize why. Then it hit me, the lab was in the same business park as the Body by Mimi corporate office.

I hadn't been back in the area since I got attacked while confronting the killer of one of my former grooms. Goosebumps appeared on my arms just driving past the building. The lab was at the other end of the business park. I found a parking spot next to Caleb's and walked inside. The building was large, made of brick with tall windows, otherwise unremarkable. As I stepped through the double doors, I spotted Caleb standing to my left in the lobby.

"Hey Jordan, right on time," Caleb said walking over to greet me.

I smiled. "I try."

"I've already let the receptionist know we're here and signed us in. Here's your visitor's badge," Caleb said handing me a sticker.

I took the sticker and placed it on the left side of my chest. "Great, thanks."

He gestured toward a grouping of chairs to the right. "Let's take a seat while we wait."

A few minutes later, a tall, slender blonde who looked like she just walked off the cover of a magazine approached us. She wore a white lab coat over a beautiful long-sleeved red dress, and heels that made my feet ache looking at them.

"Hammy!" she exclaimed striding over towards us to hug him.

"Hey Fiona, it's good to see you," Caleb replied hugging her back.

She laughed. "Call me Fi, remember silly. After that night at the conference, I think we know each other better than that."

Caleb laughed. "That was one heck of a night."

Hammy? Um hello, I'm standing right here. I wondered what kind of *night* it was. Thoughts of her and him kissing and running their hands all over each other flooded my brain. Ew, gross, I need to stop. It was not my business. I cleared my throat.

"Oh, hi! It's nice to meet you, I'm Fi," she said turning around. She stuck out her hand to shake mine.

Her grip was strong. "Leah Jordan, nice to meet you."

"Why don't you guys follow me, we'll head to my office," she instructed.

Fiona swiped her badge at the door she had come out of and led us down a long hallway. After a couple of turns, we reached her office. The plaque on the wall aside her door read: Fiona Webster, Senior Toxicologist.

"Come in, please take a seat. Caleb told me a little over the phone, but why don't you fill me in, and I'll see how I can help," she instructed.

"Thank you," I said.

"I'll let Leah give you a little background on the case. I'm just assisting her," Caleb responded.

"I'm a wedding planner and my business held a bridal show. One of our vendors, a bridal dress shop owner was found dead and one of our other vendors and family friend has been accused of the murder. The police have determined that the victim was poisoned. From what we've learned, the poison was potentially either foxglove or larkspur," I explained.

"So, what can I help with?" Fiona asked.

"I guess first we need more about each of them and how accessible they are," I said.

"Foxglove and larkspur are both common nature-made poisons. Foxglove contains digoxin, which is used to treat people with heart conditions. However, given an excessive amount, it can cause fatal results," Fiona explained.

"What type of heart conditions does it treat?" Caleb asked.

"Normally, digoxin is used to treat people with a history of heart attacks," she replied.

"What would happen to someone who wasn't supposed to be taking the medication?" Caleb asked.

"Their heart rate would be irregular or slow down. The person may experience gastrointestinal issues, headaches, weakness, and blurred vision."

"That doesn't sound pleasant," I murmured.

"Poisons are probably one of the worst ways to die. Depending on the poison, you can suffer for quite some time before the actual death occurs," Fiona said.

"Where do you find foxglove?" Caleb asked.

"You can find it pretty much anywhere. Is there a reason the police think your family friend would have the means to obtain the poison?" Fiona asked.

"She's a florist," I replied.

"Okay, I can see how they made that conclusion. However, with its accessibility, that seems a little bit like railroading her," Fiona commented.

"There is another individual we're looking into who could

have access to plants and flowers. He's a landscaper," I said.

"That seems a little more plausible to me. Those types of people are out more in the community and nature," Fiona said.

"How do they detect poison in someone's system?" I asked.

"There are different methods. We can draw blood, test hair samples, and test vitreous fluid," Fiona replied.

"Vitreous fluid?" I asked.

"I'm not sure you want to know what that is Jordan," Caleb said.

Fiona laughed. "You're looking a little green sweetie. Bringing back memories from the conference?"

Caleb shuddered. "You should have had a warning or disclaimer before that slide."

Fiona shrugged. "Who knew a room full of grown, mostly men would be so affected."

The little back-and-forth banter was a little annoying. I looked at Caleb, then back at Fiona. "Will someone just tell me what it is?"

"Vitreous fluid is found in your eyeball. When someone dies, you inject a needle into the eyeball and draw up fluid that can be tested," Fiona explained.

Oh my god. Blech. "Yeah, I shouldn't have asked."

"There can be some issues with some poisons as they are not detectable on standard tests. Is there anything else you would like to know?" Fiona asked.

"I think you've given us good information and a lot to think about," Caleb said.

"Yes, thank you for your time. It's been enlightening," I agreed.

"Not a problem. If you guys need anything else, let me know. I'll walk you both back to the front," Fiona said.

We arrived back up front, I shook her hand, and then she gave Caleb one of those way too long, intimate types of hugs. I just shook it off. Caleb and I walked out together.

"She's pretty great, isn't she?" Caleb asked.

"Yep. She's a peach," I responded.

Caleb stopped and turned around. "Are you okay Jordan?"

Crap. That sounded catty. "I'm sorry. I'm just tired and have a lot on my mind."

His face grew with concern. "Oh, okay. Is there anything I can do to help?" he asked.

"No, I'll be fine. I should get back to the office. Tomorrow is the appointment with Emilio and there is some research I still need to do," I replied.

"Good idea. I'm going to keep looking through the vehicle records. I'll let you know if I find anything," Caleb said.

"Sounds great. I'll fill you in after my appointment," I replied.

CHAPTER FOURTEEN

The rest of the day went slowly. I made some more calls and started brainstorming name ideas for the newsletter. Tales from the Bliss, Bliss Notes, and Bliss Chronicles were the best I could come up with. None were tripping my trigger except Tales from the Bliss. I'd have to wait and see what the other girls came up with.

My intercom buzzed. "Leah, please, I need you to come up front," Sally said.

"On my way," I replied.

Her voice had a sense of urgency, so I hustled up front. "Sally, what's going on? Is everything okay?"

Sally pointed. "Someone's here to see you."

I finally glanced to my left. Luke Strickland stood in the lobby, and he didn't look happy.

I smiled. "Hey Luke, it's nice to see you. What's going on?"

His stance was rigid, and he didn't even smile. "We need to talk. Now."

Oh crap. "Why don't we go to my office?" I suggested.

"Lead the way," Luke replied.

As we headed towards the hallway, I looked over at Sally and mouthed the words, 'What's all this about?' Sally just shrugged her shoulders.

I motioned for Luke to have a seat, closed my office door, and took a seat across from him at my desk. He crossed his arms and stared at me.

"Everything okay?" I asked tentatively.

"No, no it's not. Why did you lie to me the other night, Leah?" Luke asked.

Oh man, I didn't think he would find out. "What do you mean?"

"I asked you if you were snooping, looking into what happened to Vanessa Mitchell and you said no. Come to find out, that's not the truth."

"I didn't lie exactly. I just omitted the truth." I shrugged.

"That's the same thing. Don't you know how dangerous this can be? You're dealing with someone who has killed another human being."

"Caleb's been helping me. I'm fine."

"Then why did we receive a complaint?" Lucas asked.

Crap. "From whom?" I asked.

"Ed Garver. He insists you are harassing him. He stated you're following him."

"What? I did no such thing! I talked to him about his relationship with Ms. Mitchell. He cooperated of his own free will."

"So, you didn't follow him to Trinity Baptist Church last night?"

I shook my head. "I did not. It was just a coincidence."

"It was just a coincidence that you were at a meeting for people suffering from PTSD?"

"I was there to scope out the facilities!" I exclaimed.

Luke raised an eyebrow. "At six, in the evening?"

"Um...well. I wasn't ready to go home, and I was in the area, so I decided to check it out."

"Where were you before that?"

"Working."

"You weren't working. I asked Meg."

Darn. He was good. "Okay, fine. I've been investigating."

"I knew it. You aren't any better at lying than the time you, Meg, and Chelsea broke my boombox, tried hiding it, and then told me someone must have broken into my room and done it."

I sighed out loud. "That was years ago. We were dumb kids. That's hardly the same thing."

"Exactly my point. I told you how dangerous it can be to

stick your nose in other people's business. Don't you think if they hurt one person, they won't hurt others?"

"I'm fine. It's going fine. Look, why are you so concerned anyway? Are you afraid I'm doing such a good job, that I'll make the department look bad?" I asked.

Luke scoffed. "No, that wouldn't happen. I am talking not only about your safety, but your freedom. You are lucky I dissuaded Mr. Garver not to file charges."

"He was going to file charges, seriously?" I asked.

"Yes," Luke replied.

Maybe it will smooth things over if I tell him about confirming Fannie's alibi. "I do have some good news. Fannie is innocent. She was home at the time of Vanessa's murder. I have the proof."

He cocked his head and scrunched up his face. "I'm listening."

I pulled out my notes and a copy of the pizza order receipt. I handed them over.

He skimmed over the papers and looked up. "How did you get this?"

"I spoke with Fannie, and she remembered ordering a pizza from Tony's. Caleb and I went to Tony's to talk to them. They confirmed an order from her the night of the murder. Mr. Biscardi provided us with a copy of the receipt. I followed up with him, and he verified he delivered a pizza to her house."

"We'll need to follow proper procedures with this evidence. If what you have found is true, then she would be eliminated as a suspect," he explained. "But you need to leave the investigation alone. Let us do our jobs."

He didn't remember who he was talking to. Once I got involved in trying to resolve an issue, I was determined to see it to the end. "I'll make you a deal. No more getting in trouble, but I'm not stopping investigating."

Luke groaned. "You just want to drive me crazy, don't you?"

"I don't understand why you care so much. It's not like you care for me as more than a friend," I said.

He grew extremely quiet.

Before he could respond, there was a knock on my office door. The door opened quietly, it was Sally.

She looked at both of us. "I'm sorry. Did I interrupt something?"

I cleared my throat. "No, not at all. I think Luke was getting ready to leave. Right, Luke?"

He nodded his head. "Right. I'll talk to you later Leah. Just think about what I said."

Once Luke left, Sally looked at me. "Are you sure everything is okay?"

"It's fine. Nothing to worry about. What can I help you with?" I asked.

"You remember that woman who was here protesting the

other day?" Sally asked.

"Yes, why?"

"My girlfriend Sylvia just called. That woman is having a one-woman protest/sit-in at the Grand Lush Bridal Salon. She saw her when she was driving by."

"Oh jeez. That's not good," I murmured.

"Have you talked to her since the bridal show?" Sally asked.

"No, not since that day. I probably should," I replied.

"Maybe you can talk some sense into her. You've always been level-headed."

"I don't know about that. At least lately. Most people would think I'm pretty nuts for investigating another murder."

"Point taken. She could probably use a friend. Plus, you could figure out if she hurt Vanessa," Sally suggested.

"Fine. I'll at least drive over and see if she's still there. If nothing else, a bad experience with a business is not worth getting arrested over," I replied.

"Be careful. Call if you need help," Sally instructed.

Driving over to the Grand Lush Bridal Salon, I wasn't sure what I would say or do. The last time I talked to Tori

Matthews, you couldn't reason with her. Approaching the store, sure enough there she was pacing back and forth. Dressed in the same shirt she wore the day of the bridal show, she also carried the same sign.

"Ms. Matthews?" I called as I got closer.

"It's Mrs. Matthews," she replied not missing a step.

"Do you remember me? My name is Leah Jordan. We met at the bridal show at the Wedded Bliss," I asked.

She stopped and stared at me. "You're the one who called the cops on me!"

"I did. I'm sorry, but you were trespassing on private property, and we had people coming to an event. It wasn't the appropriate place for your protest," I explained.

"I just wanted to get her attention. I was desperate," Tori explained.

"I empathize. I would want to be listened to and get some resolution."

Tori stuck her chin out. "Exactly."

"What happened after you left the bridal show that day?"

"I got released a few hours later and I went home."

"Have you seen Ms. Mitchell since the bridal show?"

"No! Still nothing, that's why I'm here. I've been waiting for her to come out, but I haven't seen her," Tori grumbled.

I gave her a weird look. "You haven't heard?"

"Heard what?"

"Ms. Mitchell was murdered Saturday night."

Tori's mouth dropped. "What? Are you sure?"

The news seemed to sink in, and the color drained from her face.

"Are you okay?" I asked.

"Wow, just wow. I know I despised her, but that's awful," Tori murmured.

"You didn't go anywhere after you got home Saturday?"

"No. My husband made us dinner and then we binge-watched Netflix. I was so drained from everything that happened that I ended up passing out."

"Would your husband corroborate that?" I asked.

A look of shock came over her face. "Are you trying to accuse *me* of killing her?"

"You seem to have a pretty big vendetta against her," I replied.

Tori scoffed. "I just wanted my money back and to warn others. For them to take responsibility for their wrongs."

"People have killed for less," I commented.

Tori began crying. "I couldn't hurt a fly. Plus, I'm...I'm... Why would I put myself in that situation?"

She was hiding something. "You didn't finish your one sentence. You're what?"

Her shoulders slumped. "I'm pregnant. I found out on our honeymoon. I haven't told anyone yet because it's so early and we already lost a baby before we were married. Why would I put myself in a situation where my baby would be born in jail?"

She had a good point. "I see what you're saying. Congratulations. Don't you think that you should let this go now? Stress can't be good for the baby. I think you've gotten your message across. All you can do now is move on and look forward to your next chapter."

Tori sniffled. "You're right. My husband has been telling me the same thing. I was just being stubborn because I was so hurt, and these pregnancy hormones are no joke. Your wedding dress is supposed to be special and perfect."

"Why don't you go to Bonnie's Bakery? Tell them I sent you and get some of her famous chocolate turnovers. Buy some for you and your hubby. They're delicious!" I suggested.

Tori wiped her eyes and nose. "That's a good idea. I have had a big, sweet tooth recently. I hope that whoever hurt Ms. Mitchell gets brought to justice."

"You're welcome. Sometimes you just need to get an outside perspective."

Tori nodded her head. "Is it okay if I give you a hug?"

This was getting a little weird, but Aunt Sissy always taught me to be kind to others. "Sure."

I made sure Tori she got back to her car and headed back to mine.

CHAPTER FIFTEEN

When I arrived at the Wedded Bliss and stepped inside, Chelsea, Meg, and Sally were waiting.

"Oh, thank god!" Sally exclaimed holding her hands to her chest.

"How'd it go with Miss Crazy Pants?" Chelsea asked.

Meg smacked her on the arm. "Chelsea! That's not funny! Leah, are you okay?"

Chelsea sighed. "Sorry."

"I'm fine guys. I talked to her and convinced her to stop protesting and cut her losses," I responded.

"Talking to her worked?" Sally asked.

"It did. I just reasoned with her. Like we do with bridezillas," I explained.

Everyone laughed.

"Did you learn anything interesting?" Chelsea asked.

I waved my hand in a so-so motion. "Mostly a repeat of the beef she had against Vanessa's shop. She may be unstable, but I think she has good intentions."

"Do you think she's the one who killed Vanessa?" Meg asked.

"I don't think so. I need to verify her alibi, but she has a pretty good reason not to," I replied.

"Such as?" Sally asked.

"Tori Matthews is pregnant," I replied.

Everyone gasped.

"That could explain her behavior, pregnancy hormones can make you think and feel crazy," Meg replied.

"I'll take your word for it. Now that you know I'm fine, we can all get back to work now," I said.

"Yes ma'am," Chelsea said.

"Meg, can I talk to you for a minute?" I asked.

"Of course, what's up?" Meg asked.

"Let's go to my office," I suggested.

Meg followed me and I shut the door behind us.

Meg cocked her head and looked at me. "Am I in trouble? You've gotten very quiet and have a weird look on your face."

I shook my head. "Oh no, you are not in trouble. It's something that's playing on my mind."

"Okay, whew! Not that I was worried, but you never know. What's going on?" Meg asked.

"I don't know how to say this. Promise not to freak out, okay?"

Meg sat up straighter in her chair. "Okay."

I let out a deep breath and started talking fast. "I think Luke might like me."

Meg groaned. "That's what you needed to talk to me about?"

"Yes! Isn't that crazy?" I exclaimed.

"Where have you been? I've known my brother has had a thing for you for years. You don't need to be a psychic to see that."

I shook my head, "Wait, what? For years?"

Meg smacked her palm against her forehead. "Are you really this oblivious?"

I sighed. "I guess so."

"You were the one friend he always asked about when he came home from college. Luke always played it off as just making small talk, but I knew it was more than that. He was so happy when you came back to run the Wedded Bliss," Meg explained.

"He told you that?" I asked.

"He didn't have to. When he's around you, he just gets this goofy look on his face."

"Hmm."

"What makes you bring it up?"

"Luke stopped by my house the other night to check on me. He asked me if I was investigating. I lied and told him I wasn't. He told me he was glad I wasn't because it was dangerous. Well, that blew up in my face because the landlord Vanessa rented her shop from wanted to file charges against me for harassing him last night," I explained.

"Excuse me? Harassment?" Meg exclaimed.

I raised my hand. "Long story, I'll fill you in later. Anyway, Luke was dead set against me investigating. Eventually, I asked him something like, 'Why are you so concerned? It's not like you like me."

"What did he say?" Meg asked.

"He got quiet and didn't have a chance to respond because Sally came to tell me about Tori Matthews," I explained.

"Is it such a bad thing?"

"Huh? What?"

Meg rolled her eyes and shook her head. "The fact that Luke likes you, duh."

"Oh, that. Well, kind of. I also think Caleb likes me. Luke is a great guy, but I never thought he would like someone like me," I replied.

"Someone like you? Come on now. Stop being so hard on yourself. You are smart, beautiful and if memory serves me right, you had a crush on my brother at one point too."

If I couldn't admit it to myself, I wasn't going to admit it to anyone else just yet.

"I did, I do, I don't know."

"I think you do know, and you just don't want to accept that a guy likes you, let alone two guys," Meg replied.

I sighed. "What do I do?"

"Just let things happen and go with the flow. No one says you need to choose one over the other. Get to know them both, then decide."

"I did have a good time on that blind date a few months ago with Luke," I said.

"See?" Meg replied.

"Nothing came of it, at least not yet. On the other hand, I've had a great time working with Caleb the past few months too."

"Don't stress about it. Focus on the investigation and the business."

"Easier said than done," I murmured.

"You can do this. You're already working so hard to clear Fannie's name. See it through," Meg suggested.

I nodded. "You're right. Whatever is meant to happen with Luke or Caleb will happen, but I need to focus on the investigation."

"Right. Do you feel any better now?"

"A little. Thank you for talking to me. It just caught me off guard," I said.

"Oh stop, how many times have you listened to me go on

and on about problems I'm having? We're friends. That's what we're here for," Meg replied.

"Thanks."

We both stood up and hugged.

After some online research, I came up with a list of 'ideas' to discuss with Emilio. Next up was picking out a more provocative outfit than I would normally wear. If he was a big flirt, I was going to play along. I found my lowest-cut top and paired it with some nice blue jeans and a pair of black ballet flats. To complete my look, I put on eyeliner, eye shadow and, put my hair up in a French twist.

By the time I was done, I was exhausted. How did women do this much primping every day? I was glad it was not my daily routine. Sleeping in till the last minute was more valuable. Checking the clock, it was only nine forty-five. I had plenty of time to grab another cup of coffee while waiting.

Ten o'clock came and went. Finally, a pickup, as Mrs. Di-Carlo described, pulled into my driveway at ten-twenty. The driver's side door opened and the most muscular, tan man I'd ever seen was walking up to me. He was about 6'2", with short shaved black hair, chocolate brown eyes, and muscle for days. No wonder the women went ga-ga over him.

Once he got closer, he looked awful. He had big bags under his eyes, and it seemed like his mind was elsewhere. I opened the door and welcomed him in.

"Good morning. I'm sorry I'm late. My last appointment ran a little over. I'm Emilio Perez, it's nice to meet you. I understand you're interested in getting some landscaping done?" he asked.

"Nice to meet you too. Please have a seat. I made a list of possible projects I had in mind," I replied.

"That's great. Most people aren't always so prepared," Emilio commented.

"Thanks. Have you been in the business a long time?" I asked.

"About eight years, give or take," he replied.

"What made you decide to get into the field?" I asked.

"I just kind of stumbled into it honestly. It started out as a summer job when I was in college and been doing it ever since," Emilio responded.

I picked up the 'list' from the end table next to my chair and handed it to him. "Here's some of the ideas I came up with."

Emilio took the list and skimmed it. "These are all jobs we would be able to handle. I'll need to take some measurements and figure out a list of supplies and then we can work up a quote.”

“That sounds good. How soon do you think you’ll be able to start work and how long will it take to complete?” I asked.

Emilio didn’t reply. When I looked over at him, he was staring off and tears had formed in his eyes.

“Are you okay?” I asked.

Emilio wiped his eyes. “I’m sorry. It’s just been a rough time lately. My girlfriend recently passed away. I noticed the painting on your wall. It made me think of her.”

I looked across the room to see what painting he was talking about. It was a painting of a beautiful wedding dress given to me by a former bride as a thank you. I can see how it must have triggered him.

“I’m so sorry. Were you two together a long time?” I asked.

“About six months but it was one of those things where you know you’ve met your soulmate,” Emilio replied.

“You were very lucky. Not too many find their true soulmate. Not to pry, was her passing unexpected?”

Emilio sniffed. “It’s ok, it was very unexpected. They think she was murdered.”

“Oh my gosh. I’m so sorry,” I replied.

“Thank you. I hope the son of a…er, gun that did it gets caught. I should have been there to prevent it.” Emilio’s shoulders dropped, and he hung his head down.

“You can’t be so hard on yourself. If you keep dwelling on

the what ifs, it will make you crazy."

"I guess you're right. I'm sorry, for not being very professional today," Emilio apologized.

I waved my hand at him. "Don't worry about it. You've got a lot on your mind right now."

"Thank you for listening. I don't usually open up to strangers."

"I guess I've just given off that vibe where people are comfortable confiding in me. In school, I joked that that 'Dear Abby' must have been tattooed on my forehead."

Emilio cracked a little smile. "I should get busy on those measurements."

"Is there anything else you need from me?" I asked.

"Not right now, thank you. I'll take the measurements, head back to the office and we should be able to have a quote ready for you in the next few days. Let me get you a business card in case you have any further questions."

"Sounds great. Thank you. I look forward to hearing from you," I replied.

Emilio headed outside to get started. I let out a long breath. It went a little differently than I imagined. I'm not sure what I was expecting. Emilio was a big ladies' man, but he was a broken man.

CHAPTER SIXTEEN

The longer I sat there in my front room, the more my stomach began hurting. I realized I needed to ask Emilio more questions. Looking outside, Emilio was still measuring one of the front beds. I got up and headed outside. Approaching him, I cleared my throat.

Emilio jumped. "Hi, sorry I didn't see you there. I'm almost finished and will be on my way."

"It's okay. I need to talk to you," I said.

Emilio stood up and brushed off his hands. "Of course."

Wringing my hands, I wasn't sure how he would take my next statement. "I brought you here under false pretenses and I'm sorry."

Emilio's face scrunched up. "What? Why? I don't know what you've heard, but I don't sleep with my clients."

I started waving my hands frantically. "Oh no, no, no. That's not where I was going. Let's go inside and I'll explain everything."

Emilio followed me back inside and took a seat. "What is going on? Who are you?"

"My name really is Leah Jordan, but I'm not looking for landscaping services. I'm looking into what happened to Vanessa," I explained.

"Why didn't you just tell me..." Emilio's voice trailed off as if he made the connection.

"It's complicated," I said.

"You think I'm a suspect!" Emilio exclaimed as he tensed up.

"Everyone's a suspect right now," I replied.

"I confided in you, I cried. Now I feel like an idiot," Emilio grumbled.

"No, please, I just wanted to get to know you. Everything I said was genuine," I replied.

"You do have other suspects, right? Why are you investigating? How do you even know Vanessa?" Emilio asked.

"Slow down, one question at a time. Yes, there are other suspects. I met Vanessa when she became a vendor at my company's bridal show."

Emilio's eyebrows raised. "You're not a cop?"

"No, I'm working on this privately. Can you tell me a little about your relationship with Vanessa?" I asked.

"We met when I came over for a landscaping consultation. We talked about traveling and New York. I have family there and she used to live there. Then each time I was there, we would talk. She would bring out fresh lemonade and the friendship turned into more."

"You knew she had a boyfriend?"

Emilio let out a deep breath. "I didn't at first, then I did later. Vanessa told me that he was mean and abused her. She also told me he had a bad gambling problem. I was never at the house when he was around. After a while, she and I fell in love. Vanessa promised me she was leaving him but had to get things set up, so her business was protected," Emilio explained.

"Did you two have plans for the future?" I asked.

"Nothing definite, but yes, we began planning our future."

"When was the last time you saw Vanessa?"

"Saturday after the bridal show. We went out to dinner, had some drinks and then I dropped her off at her house," Emilio said.

"Did you talk to her after you returned to your place?" I asked.

"Yeah, well I texted her. Vanessa said she was tired and was going to relax. One of my friends, Scott, called and asked me to meet him and some other guys out for drinks. I told Vanessa I was going and would talk to her in the morning. I never talked to her again." Emilio laid his head in his hands.

"Could I have the contact info for Scott and the other guys

you met with that night?"

"Yes. I already gave that information to the police, but whatever I can do to help."

"I appreciate it. Do you know anyone who might have something against Vanessa?" I asked.

"Besides her boyfriend? No, not that I know of," Emilio said.

"Did you ever meet Vanessa's boyfriend?"

"Once, maybe twice?"

"What happened the first time?"

"It was very brief. I was leaving as he arrived home. Vanessa told him I was just there cutting the grass," Emilio explained.

"Mr. Walker wasn't suspicious?"

"Not then. A couple of weeks ago, I received a call from a blocked number and I'm pretty sure it was him. The person on the line said, 'I know what you've been doing. Leave. Her. Alone.' Then the line went dead."

"Did you tell Vanessa about the phone call?" I asked.

"Yes, but she just blew it off and told me to stop being so paranoid." Emilio shrugged.

"Was Vanessa different in the days leading up to her passing?"

"Not really. Wait, she was feeling sick now that I think of it. We went out to our favorite Sushi restaurant Asian Palace. The next day she got sick and couldn't stay out of the bathroom.

We just chalked it up to food poisoning."

"Did you also feel ill?" I asked.

"No, but I didn't have sushi either. I had General Tso's chicken," Emilio replied.

"Is there anything else you can think of that would be important?"

"Not right now, but if I do, I'll let you know."

"That would be great. Can you give me the names of the friends you went out with the other night and their contact info, please?" I asked.

"Of course. Do you have a piece of paper? I'll write it down for you," Emilio replied.

Once he finished, he handed me back the paper. After assuring Emilio I would keep doing my best to find Vanessa's killer, we said our goodbyes and he left. The girls came out of wherever they had been hiding and took their perspective places back on the couch in the front window.

Forgetting I was still dolled up, it was no wonder Chef Stefan whistled when I headed into the kitchen at The Wedded Bliss Kitchen later that morning to grab more sugar for the coffee station. Walking past the large glass door cooler, I stopped and did a double take. I looked like I was ready for a night at the club. Back in my office, I grabbed a pack of wet wipes from my desk drawer and removed the makeup. Once, I felt more like myself, I got to work.

The other day, I promised Caleb, I would fill him in on my meeting with Emilio. However, I wanted to make more phone calls and tie up a few loose ends. The first was reaching out to Tori Matthews's husband. Pulling out my notebook, it took a couple minutes to find the right notes. Picking up my desk phone, I dialed the number and began doodling on a scrap of paper while I waited.

Finally, on the fourth ring, he picked up. "Matthews, can I help you?"

"Good afternoon, Mr. Matthews, my name is Leah Jordan. I know your wife, Tori. I'm not sure if she told you I'd be reaching out?"

"Oh, the wedding show lady, right, right. I remember now," Mr. Matthews said.

Wedding show lady, I had to chuckle. I've been called worse. "Right, that's me. I need to know if you can attest that Tori was with you all night on Saturday and didn't leave the room or your sight."

"Yes. We arrived from dinner that night and she passed out next to me on the couch while we watched movies."

"Great," I replied.

"Is there anything else you need?" Mr. Matthews asked. "I'd be glad to help. You don't know how thankful I am that someone finally got through to her about the dress fiasco and the vendetta she had against that dress shop."

Aww, that was nice to hear. "You're welcome, but I didn't do anything. I just tried to get her to see things differently. How's she doing?"

"Doing good. She's focusing all her energy on getting ready for the baby."

"I'm glad I could help. Thank you for letting me take a few minutes of your time Mr. Matthews, I appreciate it," I said.

"Of course. Thank you. Have a good day," Mr. Matthews replied before disconnecting the call.

I made an air checkmark. Another person of interest was off the list. Ed Garver, Fannie, and Tori were in the clear. That left Emilio, Annie, and Hoyt. Talking to Annie and Hoyt didn't set off alarms, but with more information from Emilio, it was a good idea to revisit them.

My cell phone rang. It was Caleb. "Hey, I was just going to call you. What's up?"

"I've narrowed down the car list to a handful of possibilities. Finally!" Caleb explained.

Awesome news. "That's great."

"How did it go with Emilio?"

"Not bad. I ended up giving up my ruse because I needed more info from him," I said.

"Was he mad?" Caleb asked.

"More like confused. He was an emotional wreck. Remember that wedding dress painting on my wall in the front room? He caught sight of it, and it triggered him."

"Poor guy. What kind of information did you learn?"

"A good one. He was head over heels for Vanessa. Pretty easy on the eyes, I see why all the girls liked him," I said.

Caleb cleared his throat. "Do you think he hurt Vanessa? Jealousy is an ugly monster."

"No. He has an alibi. I was just going to call and verify it with the people he was with, then you called."

"I'm surprised. I figured he would be a prick. Time will tell. Do you have time to meet up? I thought we could go and canvass the last five cars from the list I narrowed down."

"That sounds good. I was able to verify Tori Matthews alibi and clear her, so she's no longer a suspect," I said.

"Good job, Jordan. Why don't I come pick you up, we could grab a bite to eat, and we can talk more while we drive around?" Caleb suggested.

"Sounds good. I could use a big, greasy, cheeseburger. I'll buy."

"Twist my arm. Never met a burger I didn't like. See you soon Jordan."

Twenty minutes later, Caleb and I were headed to Burger Shack. A small restaurant modeled after the old-fashioned car hop joints from the sixties. It'd been a mainstay in town for years. In high school on Friday nights, everyone would go there after the home football games. They also had some of the best shakes in the Midwest.

Caleb pulled up to one of the ordering lanes. We both took a few minutes to peruse the menu.

"Know what you want?" I asked.

"I'm ready if you are," Caleb replied.

I nodded. "Yep. Go ahead and hit the button."

"Welcome to Burger Shack, home of the colossus burger. What can I get for you today?" the employee asked over the speaker.

"We need a number two double burger combo with a regular pop, and..." Caleb turned to look at me for me to go next.

"A number one burger combo with a strawberry shake," I called out.

"Can I get you anything else?" she asked.

"No thank you, that's all," Caleb replied.

The food arrived a few minutes later and we both dug in. Forget a salad, a good, juicy burger is the best, especially with cheese, mayo, and ketchup. I took a few bites before I touched any of my French fries.

Caleb moaned. "Mm. This is so, so good!"

I stifled a giggle. "You've got a little ketchup on your mouth."

Caleb started wiping his mouth. "Did I get it?"

Laughing, I shook my head no. Reaching out towards Caleb, I grabbed his right hand and moved it to the correct area. The minute my hand touched his, it was like a static shock. I quickly pulled my hand back, grabbed a few of my fries, and shoved them into my mouth.

Caleb had a grin on his face. "Thanks, Jordan."

My mouth was still full of fries, so I just nodded. We finished the rest of our meal in silence. Once Caleb was finished, he pulled a folder from his bag in the backseat.

"Here's the list left from what I could narrow down."

"Did any of them have a connection to our suspects?" I asked.

"Not that I've been able to determine so far," Caleb replied.

"Where do we start?"

"The first on the list is Kristal Evans. Figured we would go by the address and see if the owners are home."

"I'm ready, let's roll," I said.

We drove over to an older neighborhood on the west side of town. Arriving at the address, we noticed the black sedan we were looking for was not in the driveway, but a mini-SUV was present. Caleb walked up to the porch first and I followed. He knocked on the door.

A female in her forties opened the door. "Hello, can I help you?"

"Good afternoon, ma'am. We were looking for Kristal Evans. Is she home by chance?" Caleb asked.

"That's me," the woman replied.

"Great. Do you have a few minutes to talk?" I asked.

She gave a pointed look. "I suppose so, why?"

"Can you tell me where you were last Saturday?" Caleb asked.

The woman scrunched her face up. "Before I answer, can you tell me what is regarding?"

"A black four-door Chevrolet sedan was witnessed in the area before a crime and we're trying to locate the vehicle and its owner."

"It wasn't my car. My daughter drives that car, and is attending college in North Carolina," Ms. Evans replied.

Cross that one off the list. We thanked Ms. Evans for her time and moved on to the next address. The next few addresses were dead ends as well. One was out of commission and hadn't been driven in months, and another, the last person was working in Columbus at one of the hospitals at the time of Vanessa's murder.

"This is like hunting for the needle and we're drowning in the hay," I muttered.

"There are still a couple left. Let's see what happens," Caleb replied.

CHAPTER SEVENTEEN

"Plug the next address into the map app, please. Who are we talking to?" Caleb asked.

"Michael Weiss, LLC. A business?" I replied.

Hmm, it could be a fleet vehicle," Caleb replied.

As we approached the address, we were pulling up to a buy here, pay here, car lot. Located at the corner of Hanson and Lark, there were approximately twenty vehicles. A modular trailer sat at the back and served as the office. Most of the cars looked like they had seen better days. I was no expert, but some of the prices on their windows seemed like highway robbery.

Caleb parked in an open spot on the left side of the office. We ascended the stairs and entered. A small sitting area was to the right and what appeared to be a secretary desk sat in the middle facing us near a small hallway. As we approached, we heard talking coming from the back.

"You've already paid and it's past the fifteen-day return date. I'm sorry. No, there's nothing that can be done. Yes, we do inspect our vehicles when they arrive. Just tell them they can come buy another of our cars, but we are not refunding their money," the male voice stated.

A few minutes later, the guy walked out from the back. He was about five foot seven, with greasy-looking medium-length brown hair, and a mustache. The shape of his face reminded me of a mouse or weasel. He wore a white dress shirt, and khakis and wore enough cologne to choke a horse.

He stuck his hand out. "Sorry folks, I didn't realize anyone was here. Looking for a new car? I've got a few real beauties out there. The name's Mike, Mike Weiss."

Caleb reached out and shook his hand. "Caleb Hamilton. We're interested in a car, just not one for sale."

Mr. Weiss's brow furrowed in confusion. "Not exactly sure what you mean sir."

"I'm looking for a black 4-door Chevrolet sedan. It was witnessed near a crime scene. After reviewing vehicle records, you were listed as owning one," Caleb explained.

"I have a few black sedans. Why don't you come into my office, and we can discuss this in private," Mr. Weiss suggested.

The office, if you could call it that, was a disaster. Wood paneling flanked the walls, and an ugly pea-green carpet covered the floor. In the center of the room sat a large, old-fashioned gray metal desk, flanked by two black metal four-drawer file cabinets, each topped with stacks of folders. More piles of files rested at either end of the desk. Two metal banquet chairs faced the desk, their pleather seats cracked and patched up with duct tape.

"What kind of crime was the car involved in?" Mr. Weiss asked.

"Murder," I replied.

Mr. Weiss sat up straight in his chair. "Whoa, whoa, whoa! Now that's some serious stuff. I don't think I want to be wrapped up in that."

"A little late for that I'm afraid," I replied.

"Maybe we should just give his information to the authorities and let them dig into it. I am sure they would be interested in learning all the ins and outs of your business," Caleb replied.

Mr. Weiss's face went white. "No, no, I don't think that will be necessary. I'll do whatever I can to help."

"Thank you, much appreciated," Caleb said.

"Do you happen to have a registration number or license plate number for the vehicle you are looking for?" Mr. Weiss asked.

"I do. The license number is BX123WY," Caleb replied.

Mr. Weiss went to the old computer sitting on his desk and began typing. "Okay, I found it."

"Do you have the vehicle on the lot?" Caleb asked.

"I'll have to check. That vehicle is in my rental fleet," Mr. Weiss explained.

"You rent out some of your vehicles?" I asked.

"Used cars are my main business, but after the recession, I decided to expand my income streams," Mr. Weiss replied.

"Do you keep contracts on your rental cars?" Caleb asked.

"Of course, let me see if I can find it," Mr. Weiss replied.

"That would be great," I said.

He began rifling through the pile of folders to his left. It must not have been there because he re-stacked the folders. Then he grabbed a folder from the bottom of the right pile.

"Ah-ha! Here we go," he said as he opened the folder.

The folder was a mishmash of pieces of paper. How this guy stayed in business was beyond me.

"Now what dates were you looking for?" Mr. Weiss asked.

"Last Saturday, the 15th," Caleb responded.

Mr. Weiss flipped through a few slips of paper and finally pulled one from the pile. "Yes, the black Chevrolet sedan was rented to a Hoyt Walker. Does that name mean anything?"

Caleb and I both looked at each other.

"You're sure?" I asked.

Mr. Weiss picked the paper up and showed it to us. "That's what it says."

Sure enough, at the bottom right of the paper scrawled was 'Hoyt Walker'.

"Do you remember renting to him?" Caleb asked.

"Oh yeah. He was a dick." Mr. Weiss quickly covered his mouth and then looked at me. "Sorry," he mumbled.

"I've heard worse," I replied.

"What do you mean he was a d-word?" Caleb asked.

"He came in all in a huff, requested a car rental, pays in all cash. Then I found the car in my lot the next morning when I came in at eight and the keys were in the locked drop box out front. The car was immaculate. Cleaned from top to bottom. That never happens," Mr. Weiss recalled.

"Do you recall if Mr. Walker mentioned why he was renting a car?" Caleb asked.

"You know, now that you ask, I was joking around asking him if he was going to Vegas for the weekend or making a trip to Niagara Falls, but all he would say is that he needed to take care of something," Mr. Weiss explained.

"Was he alone?" I asked.

"He was, but he got a call from a female while he was here. I felt sorry for her. He was being a real jerk. Ordering her to stop freaking out about something. I didn't think anything of it at the time. You know how women can be hysterical," Mr. Weiss said rolling his eyes.

I cleared my throat, then shot him a look.

Mr. Weiss's face grew red. "Present company excluded."

If I didn't already think Mr. Weiss was a scuzz ball, add

misogynist to it.

"Did he mention the woman by name?" Caleb asked.

"I don't recall hearing a name," he replied.

"Is there anything else you can remember about Mr. Weiss or the car when it was returned?" Caleb asked.

"There was one thing that was off, but I didn't think much of it. The driver's side seat was pushed up close to the steering wheel," Mr. Weiss replied.

"Was that it?" I asked.

"Yes. If you two don't have any more questions, I need to get back to business," Mr. Weiss said.

"If we have any further questions, we'll be in touch," Caleb instructed as we stood up.

We left the office, got back in his car and left the car lot.

"You know what this means right?" Caleb asked.

"That Hoyt lied to me when he said he was out of town?" I asked.

"Well, that, but also that he wasn't working alone. If the car seat was pushed up, someone else was driving the car. Mr. Walker is over six feet tall, no way it was him," Caleb replied.

Oh my gosh, he's right. "Who else could it be? Maybe Vanessa wasn't the only one with someone on the side."

"I think we should talk to Annie Price again. If she is as close to Vanessa as we've been told she would know if Vanessa suspected Hoyt of cheating and who it could be," Caleb said.

I checked my watch. "I agree. Women always tend to confide in their closest friends/allies. She should still be at the bridal shop. Let's go."

CHAPTER EIGHTEEN

We arrived at the bridal store and parked. Once we entered the store, I approached the front counter. No customers were present, and a few clerks were spread out throughout the store. I walked up to the front counter to ask for Annie.

"Good afternoon, welcome to Grand Lush Bridal Salon, were you looking for a wedding dress?" the girl asked.

I began nervously laughing. "Wha-at? Oh, no, no." I gestured back and forth between Caleb and me. "We're not getting married," I managed to stutter.

A look of disappointment came over her face. "Aww, that's too bad. You two make a lovely couple."

Caleb wrapped his arm around my waist and squeezed tight. "You are too kind. Alas, the one girl who rejects my handsome charm." He gave a wink.

The girl giggled. "Hopefully she'll change her mind."

It felt good having his arm around me. hen his hand brushed mine, it was like tiny currents of electricity zipping through my body. An unexpected rush of emotions flooded my mind.

I pulled myself away from Caleb and straightened myself up. "Is Annie Price available? We would really like to speak to her."

The girl took a minute to peel her eyes away from Caleb and realized I had spoken. "Oh Annie, sure, just a minute." She paged her and asked us to take a seat.

A few minutes later, Annie descended the staircase from the far side. Once she saw who was waiting for her, she pasted a fake smile on her face.

"Leah, so nice to see you again. How are you doing?" Annie asked.

I smiled. "Annie, it's good to see you again too. I had some follow-up questions I didn't get to ask you the other day. Do you mind if we talk in your office?"

"Of course. Who's your companion?" Annie replied.

"Caleb Hamilton at your service. I'm just helping Leah out." Caleb gently took Annie's left hand and placed a soft kiss on it.

I elbowed Caleb. "Laying it on a bit thick, don't you think?" I said through gritted teeth.

Annie blushed. "It's a pleasure to meet you, Caleb"

She led us upstairs and ushered us into her office. Caleb and

I took a seat across from her.

"Thank you for agreeing to meet with me again. I appreciate all your help," I said.

"Of course, no problem," Annie replied.

"The other day when I was here, our conversation got interrupted. I have a few more questions," I said.

"Sure, however I can help," Annie said.

"Knowing how close you were with Vanessa, did she ever suspect Hoyt was cheating on her with another woman?" I asked.

Annie looked taken aback. "Hoyt, er Mr. Walker?" No, not that she mentioned to me. Why do you ask?"

"Some new information has come to light, that she may not have been the only one seeing someone outside of the relationship," Caleb explained.

"You said during our last conversation, that the last time you saw Vanessa on Saturday was after the bridal show, correct?" I asked.

"Right. She was going out to dinner," Annie replied.

"Did Mr. Walker contact you at any point trying to locate Vanessa?" Caleb asked.'

"I don't recall. He may have. Things have been so crazy," Annie replied.

Before we could ask any more questions, there was a knock at the door. It opened and one of Annie's employees stuck her head in the door.

"Annie, it's Liza. Sorry to interrupt you, but there is an issue with one of the deliveries. Could you come down and help me please?"

Annie looked at Liza, then at us. "Excuse me, please. I'll be right back. Would you two care for some water?"

"That would be great, thank you," I replied.

"Liza, will you please grab Leah and Caleb each a glass of water and then meet me back in the receiving area?" Annie asked.

"Of course," Liza responded before leaving the room.

"I apologize again, I will return as quickly as I can," Annie said before leaving the room.

Liza returned with two lemon cucumber glasses of water in fancy plastic wine glasses. We thanked her, and then she left closing the door behind her.

"I thought you said Annie was shy and quiet?" my partner asked.

"When I first met her, it was true. Being out from under Vanessa's thumb has worked wonders," I replied.

"I guess so. I think she lied when you asked her about Hoyt having another woman," Caleb said.

"Really? How could you tell?" I asked.

"Annie looked up and to the left when she replied. A red flag," he explained.

It was. "Let's ask her about why she's lying?"

"Good idea," Caleb agreed.

We had both finished our glasses of water. I looked around for a trash can and spotted one of them behind her desk sitting slightly behind near a filing cabinet. I motioned for Caleb to hand me his cup, to toss them both in the trash. As I went to dispose of them in the can, a spot of white with writing on it caught my eye.

I turned towards Caleb. "Do you have a hankie?"

Caleb gave me a strange look. "How did you know I carried a handkerchief?"

I sighed. "Lucky guess? Just hand it over, Hamilton. I see something, but I don't want to touch it."

Caleb handed me the handkerchief and I went back over to the trash can. Wrapping the it around my hand, I dug down and pulled out the medication bottle. The patient's name was none other than Hoyt Walker. The medication was digoxin.

I gasped.

"What? What is it? Don't keep me in suspense," Caleb said.

I carried the bottle back over to Caleb. I held my hand out to show him.

"Well, I'll be damned. We got them," Caleb said.

Annie opened the door. "Sorry you two, I'm back. There was a mix up..." Her voice trailed off as she realized what I was holding. She looked at me, looked at Caleb, and took off.

"Crap! What do I do with this?" I asked, holding up the bottle.

"Wrap the handkerchief around it and place it in your bag for now. We need to catch her," Caleb instructed.

I did as Caleb suggested and we both took off after her. When we reached the top of the stairs, I could see Annie heading towards the accessories area. Caleb went down the left staircase and I went down to the right.

"Annie, stop!" I yelled as I ran towards her.

"No! Leave me alone!" Annie screamed.

Huffing and puffing, I was able to catch up to her near a display of dress shoes. It was like a game of cat and mouse. I went one way, and she went the other. This went on for what felt like forever. Annie began to laugh.

"You don't want to do this Annie. This is not you. Please don't make it worse for yourself," I pleaded.

"Oh, bite me! Do you know the years I suffered being treated like the dirt under Vanessa's shoe? When she came back from New York, she acted like she was so much better than everyone. Vanessa forgot she was just a small-town, geeky girl from Ohio," Annie seethed.

As she ranted, I decided to take a chance and lunged towards her. Annie grabbed a white high-heeled strappy sandal and chucked it at me. Before I could turn to miss it, it smacked me upside my left temple. Temporarily stunned, Annie took the opening to run.

I ran to catch up with her. She was zipping in and out of the racks of dresses. Caleb caught my attention and motioned for me to go right, and he'd go left. By the time I got around and was down a few rows, Caleb was trying to rationalize with her. She was holding a mannequin's arm as a weapon.

"Put it down Annie. Let's just talk about this. You didn't mean to do anything. If Hoyt was the one who made you do this, then you need to tell your side of the story," Caleb pleaded.

Annie was quiet for a minute, began crying, and lowered the mannequin arm. "He said it was the only way we could be together. That Vanessa was dropping me and kicking me out of the business."

While she was talking, I crept up behind her. Caleb kept her talking.

"That's awful. You did everything for her. You gave your sweat, tears, and blood," Caleb sympathized.

Annie nodded as she wiped away tears. "I did, I always did. Whatever she asked, with no appreciation."

Once I got a few feet from her, I ran full force at her and tackled her to the ground.

She began screeching and wiggling under me. "Hold still, just hold still. Caleb, call the cops," I yelled.

She continued to fight and flail. I held on for dear life until the cops showed up. Once officers arrived, they placed her in handcuffs and took her down to the station. The salesclerks, Caleb, and I were all separated and questioned. After they were finished, Caleb and I went back up to the front of the store. Then Luke walked in.

Oh crap.

"You two are free to go," Luke instructed.

"What about Hoyt Walker?" I asked.

"He's in custody now. Annie tipped him off, but when we received Caleb's call, we dispatched a couple of units to his home and they caught him loading up his car, trying to skip town," Luke explained.

I let out a long breath. "That's great news."

"Those two won't be able to harm anyone else now," Caleb agreed.

"Did you get the bottle?" I asked.

"Yes, one of the other detectives mentioned what you found, it's been packaged and sent to the station to be processed. That will be important when we go to trial. I know we've been butting heads lately but thank you for your help," Luke said.

"It's okay. You're welcome," I said.

Annie Price and Hoyt Walker were both charged and convicted. Neither of them would be seeing daylight for a very long time. No one in Vanessa's family wanted to continue running the bridal store so it was closed. Fannie was cleared of all charges, and we were all gathering to celebrate.

Chef Stefan pulled out all the stops. He prepared beef tenderloin, gruyere au gratin potatoes, roasted mixed vegetables, a mixed green salad, and cheesecake with a cherry topping. Meg, Chelsea, and Sally planned the whole event. We were in the Love room. Caleb, Luke, and Sally's new beau, Paul, also joined us.

"Everything is ready, enjoy!" Meg announced.

We all grabbed our food and found seats at the tables. Once everyone settled, Fannie stood up.

"Thank you, everyone, for believing in me, and helping clear my name. It means so much to have so many great people in my life."

"Here, here!" The room cheered raising a glass.

"Most of all, I must thank Leah who gave her all. Thank you."

"You're welcome," I responded.

As I looked around the room, my heart was full. The rest of the dinner was wonderful with laughter, good food, and conversation. Slowly everyone began leaving. Fannie, Sally, and her boyfriend left first. Chelsea, Meg and I started cleaning up while Luke and Caleb helped tear it down.

"Well, you did it again Jordan," Caleb said approaching me.

"I couldn't have done it without you. Thank you," I said.

"You're welcome. We do make a pretty great team," Caleb replied.

"What's next for you?" I asked.

"I should probably get back home. I have some cases that I need to follow up on. You?"

"I think a break would be nice. The last few weeks have been crazy with all the preparation for the Bridal show, then Vanessa's murder."

"If you want to come up my way, let me know. I'd love the company," Caleb offered.

"I'll think about it, Hamilton, thanks," I said hugging him.

When everything was finished, I gathered my stuff and shut out all the lights. I didn't know what was coming up next, but for now, things were all right in the world.

WEDDING TIPS

<u>Choosing a Venue</u>

For your wedding, deciding on a venue is one of the biggest and most important choices you will make. It will set the tone for your special day. Also, it is important to choose your venue before working on the other details.

The earlier you begin your search the better. This will allow you more time to check out all your options, and find the right one for you, and your needs. Plus make sure it is available on the date of your special day.

While it can seem overwhelming at first, determining the basic elements of your wedding will help in scaling down the options and finding the perfect one for you and your significant other.

These are some of the different factors to think about:

<u>Location</u>

In the past weddings were held in the bride's hometown. Now, the options for venues are limitless. Deciding where you want to get married, a big city or somewhere more rustic, a location that is special to you as a couple or even a destination location is the first step.

Next you want to decide if you want to hold the ceremony and the reception at the same venue. It can be convenient to use the same place for both, but some couples may prefer to hold the ceremony in a separate location and the reception elsewhere.

<u>Dates</u>

Before you go searching for venues, it is a good idea to have a date or a couple dates in mind. Depending on the popularity of a venue, the location or the time of year, they may already have several events already booked on the date you are interested in.

<u>Theme or Style</u>

Your wedding theme or overall style is another important feature to think about. If you are having a more rustic wedding, would a fancy very upscale facility be a good option, or would a barn surrounded by fields and woods be a better fit?

<u>Guest Count</u>

You also need to consider your budget. How much have you allocated for the venue? Do the ones you are looking at fit within it? Your guest count will also play an important part in locating your venue. While you do not need an exact head count, having a general idea of how many guests you plan to invite will help you find the right size venue.

Amenities

Does the facility offer in-house catering, decorating, tables, chairs and linens and even have on-site event coordinators. Do they have adequate parking and restroom facilities for your guests?

Vendor Options

Are you allowed to use your own vendors, ie. Flowers, catering, entertainment, etc or do you need to choose companies from the venue's preferred list?

Accommodations

If you plan on having guests from out of town or flying in, you need to take into consideration what is around the area of your venue. Can your guests easily locate the venue, and what accommodations are available nearby?

Accessibility

Do you have any guests with mobility issues or other special needs? Can the venue accommodate them? Are there ramps, elevators, handicapped accessible restrooms available?

Privacy

A wedding is a huge moment in your life, and you want to think about privacy. Does the venue hold multiple events at the same time? Could your ceremony or reception be interrupted by strangers or onlookers? Or how much of the place will you have to yourselves?

<u>Reviews</u>

Research the venues and look for any reviews. Pay attention to the positive and negative reviews. Check out review websites or join local wedding Facebook groups and check for any recommendations of venues that you are interested in.

Now you've chosen your possible options, what happens next?

-Set up an appointment to do a walkthrough of the different venues you are interested in.

-Do not be afraid to ask questions and be thorough when you are visiting a venue.

-Once you have visited some potential options, be sure to weigh the pros and cons before making a final decision.

-When you have made your choice, you will ask the venue for a contract.

-Be sure to review it thoroughly and ask to clarify anything that does not make sense.

-You also want to be clear that you understand the deposit and payment schedule.

-After you have reviewed the contract, you are happy with all the details, then you sign it, turn it in and you've officially booked your venue for your special day. Hooray!

<u>Décor</u>

When choosing your decor, you first want to have an idea of your overall look for your special day. Do you want glamorous, traditional, country chic or something more minimalistic? If picking one specific style is a challenge, you can also think about it from the perspective of how you want your special day to feel. Whether that's romantic, relaxed, modern, etc. Selecting a color palette for your special day will also serve as a guideline. Instead of just blue and green, expand your choices by adding different hues and coordinating colors.

Now that you have chosen a venue, it may also inspire your choices. Use your venue and the areas around it to your benefit. It can also help determine how much decor would be needed. If there is beautiful landscaping, unique architecture, then you may not need to use as much decor. Another way to gain some inspiration is to check out pictures of previous weddings at your venue or see if your wedding planner can create a mock up of different decor options. Be sure to also check with your venue and find out if they have any decor elements they supply or that can be rented or included in your contract.

You can also break your decor down into a few different categories: Functional items, Basic decor items, Secondary Items and Extras or splurges.

Functional items will be the chairs, tables, flatware, China, lighting, seating chart and or table numbers.

Basic decor items include tablecloths, centerpieces, aisle runners, aisle markers, and arches or backdrops for the ceremony and reception areas.

Secondary items would be the place cards, menu cards, wedding signage (directional, decorative, etc).

Extras or splurges are those elements that you want to add that you think will be special for your guests or elements that you really want for your special day, such as a photo booth, an elaborate arch, a candy bar, grazing tables or specially created drinks just for the wedding.

Here is a check-list to help you get started:

<u>Ceremony</u>
-Aisle markers
-Aisle runners
-Arch/Arbor
-Altar backdrops
-Altar arrangements
-Bridal party bouquets and boutonnieres
-Flower girl and ring bearer items
-Garland
-Ceremony Signage
-Programs
-Guestbook
-Welcome sign

<u>Reception</u>

-Centerpieces

-Flatware

-Glassware

-China

-Chair covers

-Tablecloths

-Napkins

-Sweetheart table

-Candelabras

-Floating candles

-String lights

-Tea lights/Votives

-Card box

-Gift table

-Cake topper

ACKNOWLEDGEMENTS

To my best friends since high school, my ride or dies. In the words of The Golden Girls, thank you for being a friend.

To all my fellow indie authors and booktokers, thank you for being such an amazing support system and community!

To Andrew, my first fan and now my friend. Thank you for all your support.

ABOUT THE AUTHOR

Small Towns. Quirky Characters. Hidden Secrets.

Christine Lawrence resides in a small town in Northwest Ohio with her husband,
stepdaughter, son and three spoiled dogs. An avid reader since childhood, she
decided to mesh her two favorite genres, romance and mystery. Working hard to
complete the next book in The Wedded Bliss mystery series, she spends her free time
participating in local writing groups, traveling and spending time with her family.
Christine has a bachelor's degree in forensic science with a specialization in Crime
Scene Investigation and a master's degree in forensic psychology. Her background
as a private investigator and obsession with all thing's crime related gives her endless
fodder for her small-town cozy mysteries.

ALSO BY CHRISTINE LAWRENCE

I Thee Dead: Book #1 in The Wedded Bliss Series

www.ingramcontent.com/pod-product-compliance
Lightning Source LLC
Chambersburg PA
CBHW032301310726
48973CB00008B/2477